Once Upon a PRINCESS

CHRISTINE MARCINIAK

CBaY Books
Dallas, Texas

Once Upon a Princess

Cover illustration by Jeff Crosby.
jeffcrosbyillustration.com

For more information, write:
CBAY Books
PO Box 670296
Dallas, TX 75367

Children's Brains are Yummy Books
Dallas, Texas
www.cbaybooks.blog

ISBN: 978-1-944821-28-9
eBook ISBN: 978-1-944821-29-6
Kindle ISBN: 978-1-944821-30-2
PDF ISBN: 978-1-944821-31-9

To Fritzi … because if she hadn't been my friend way back in kindergarten I never would have thought to name a princess after her.

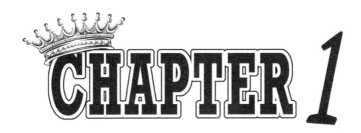

CHAPTER 1

It is going to be the most memorable night of my life.

I, Princess Fredericka, get to officially attend a royal ball and not be hustled off to bed before the dancing even starts, because today is a momentous day. On this day, October first, eight hundred years ago, our family founded Colsteinburg.

Mademoiselle Colette adds a jeweled circlet to my pinned-up red hair.

"You are much too young for a tiara," she frets, even as she makes sure it is straight.

"I'm twelve. Besides, tonight I need to look the part of a princess, wouldn't you agree?" I ask my governess.

"Georgiana didn't attend a royal ball until she was thirteen," Mademoiselle Colette points out.

Finally I get to do something that Georgiana didn't get to do!

"But how often does a country have an Octocentennial?" I ask. "I shouldn't have to miss out just because my birthday hasn't come around yet." I turn my head this way and that as I study myself in the mirror. I like the way the tiara looks. Perhaps I can convince Mam to let me wear one all the time.

I use my phone to take a picture of the full effect and upload it to social media with the caption, "Finally going to a ball."

Mademoiselle Colette sighs the put-upon sigh she's perfected over the years. "Far be it from me to tell the king and queen how to raise their younger daughter. I only work here."

I give her a hug. "But I love you, Mademoiselle. You know that. Are you going to the dance?"

"I am going to put my feet up and watch TV. That is as much excitement as I need."

So little imagination. "You should go," I say.

"Perhaps I'll go for the dinner," she says. "Now, go see if your mother approves of you."

"Mam always approves of me," I say, grinning at her.

She gives me a playful swat. "See if she approves of how you look."

I nearly get the heels of my shoes tangled in my red-and-white silk floor-length gown as I start to walk. Mademoiselle Colette steadies me and shakes her head in despair.

"You need to be in pinafores and saddle shoes."

I stick my tongue out at her and head down the thickly

carpeted hall to my parents' suite.

I knock, and the door is opened by Matilde, my mother's lady's maid. "May I see my mother, please?" I say.

"The king and queen are speaking with Mr. Frank, but you may come in and wait." I go into the anteroom with its hanging tapestries and stained glass windows. "You look lovely, Your Royal Highness," Matilde says.

"Thank you." That's one vote of approval anyway.

I hear voices coming from the adjoining sitting room, but I know better than to barge in when my parents are in a discussion with Pap's top adviser, so I sit on a cushioned bench, swinging my feet and waiting.

"Frederick, I tell you there are people poisoning the atmosphere." Ivan Frank's raised voice comes through the closed door to me. "People who do not want another year of Mohr rule in Colsteinburg, let alone another eight hundred."

Pap answers him but keeps his voice low, and his words are indistinct.

"I don't know who!" Ivan responds, loudly. "There is someone behind the unrest though, but we haven't found out who."

I've seen the letters in the paper by people who aren't happy with the way things are run, but things are run the way they always have been, and there are always people who aren't happy about it. I've paid enough attention in history class to know that. One disgruntled rabble-rouser can cause a lot of problems. I hope they find him soon and put a stop to it.

"Watch your back," Ivan continues. "Perhaps this celebration is ill advised."

A shiver runs up my own back. What does he mean by that? Does he think that with unrest in the government, people will think the celebration is foolhardy, or does he think that something bad might happen?

The door opens, and they come out, my parents in their regal attire and Ivan Frank looking dashing in his tuxedo.

"Thank you, Ivan," Pap says, his hand on his friend's shoulder. "I do not believe canceling the ball is the answer. If we were to do that, we would look afraid. I am not afraid. It would look as if we had something to fear. And we don't. Let people talk. They always have." He glances at me and lowers his voice. "And double security around the palace."

Ivan nods his head. "Yes, Sire," he says, and with a smile and nod to me, he leaves the room.

"Let's have a look at you, Fritzi," Pap says, grinning as if his adviser hadn't just been giving him bad news.

I stand up and slowly turn around so Mam and Pap can see me.

Pap only became king of Colsteinburg last year when my grandfather died. Pap wears his formal uniform with a colorful array of ribbons and badges. I don't know what all of them mean, but I do know only the king can wear them. And he's the king.

Mam's auburn hair is piled artfully on her head. Her gown is form-fitting and worthy of a Hollywood red carpet.

Next to them, I feel like a little kid playing dress-up.

"You look so grown up," Pap says with approval.

"Too grown up," Mam says. She doesn't seem quite as satisfied. "What happened to my little girl?"

"I'm not so little anymore, Mam," I say.

"No, I suppose you're not." She has a wistful tone in her voice, but I can't help growing up. In fact, I can't wait until I'm as grown up as Georgie and everyone takes me seriously.

"Is everything all right, Pap?" I ask, trying not to sound too concerned, even though Ivan's words left a bubble of anxiety in my belly. "Ivan sounded worried."

"It's Ivan's job to worry," Pap says. "Everything is fine. Are you ready for your first ball?"

His certainty bursts the worry bubble, and I feel much lighter. "Very!"

"Then let's see if Georgie's ready, and we can get this party started, what do you think?" Pap asks.

I grin back at him. "Sounds good!"

Georgie, of course, is not ready. She's eighteen and doesn't rush when she wants to look nice. When she is done, I feel like I should just fade into the woodwork. She's elegant and graceful and looks exactly how someone would expect the next-in-line to the throne to look: blonde, fresh-faced, and cheerful.

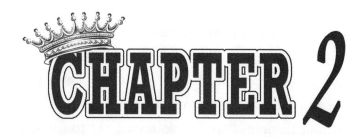

CHAPTER 2

A flock of butterflies crowds my stomach while we wait at the top of the curving stairs for the master of ceremonies to announce us. Below us, the ballroom is awash in color. Images of the red dragon of Colsteinburg are everywhere, from the white flags on the walls to the centerpieces on the tables. With so many flowers—roses in red and white and yellow, orchids in purple and pink and white, lilies in white and orange—the ballroom looks like a garden, and their fragrance fills the air. Light glints off the crystals in the chandeliers, making the room sparkle. The ladies' dresses, most borrowing their styling from the Middle Ages, are a rainbow of silken colors. The men look stunning in tuxedos, though some look even more amazing in tight breeches and colorful tunics, taking the Octocentennial theme to its next level.

A trumpet plays a fanfare, and all eyes turn up to us.

"Her Royal Highness, Princess Fredericka."

That's me.

"Go, Fritzi," Georgie whispers, giving me a tiny nudge.

Holding my head high and my back straight, in a way that would make my dancing instructor proud, I walk slowly down the wide, curved staircase. Photographers snap my picture, and I make sure to smile politely, not grin idiotically. I make it to the dais without tripping or making a fool of myself. Success! Now to wait for the rest of my family.

"Her Royal Highness, Princess Georgiana."

Georgie smiles brightly as she enters the ballroom. There's just something about my sister that makes her look regal. She joins me on the dais, and I take a deep breath. I'm not alone anymore.

"Her Majesty, Queen Cassandra."

Mam glides down the stairs, nodding acknowledgment to the people as she passes them, and joins us.

"His Majesty, King Frederick."

He smiles to the people as he strides across the ballroom floor. He was born to be king and is enjoying every minute of it.

A few violins play softly, a hint of the music to come. I'm ready for the dancing to start. That's the fun part of a ball, after all, and it's the part I always missed out on, but first the people need to come and make their obeisance to the king and queen, and by default to me and Georgie. They form a line and walk past us, bowing or curtsying as they do.

I shift from foot to foot, and my cheeks hurt from smiling, but Pap has reminded us over and over again that greeting the people in a respectful manner is part of the responsibility of being the royal family, so I nod and say hello and greet people by name when I know them.

Prince Etienne of Lothringen appears in the line, and I glance at my sister to see her reaction. There's not much that can fluster her, but Prince Etienne always makes her blush. Tall and slender, with light brown hair and eyes, he looks like he could be central casting's choice for Prince Charming. They're to be married in three years, when she turns twenty-one. It's been arranged since they were three. Sure, the whole thing is political, but they don't care because they are crazy about each other and always have been.

No one has bothered to arrange a marriage for me.

It's not as important, I guess, because I'm not next in line for the throne.

Prince Etienne smiles at me, and I get a strange weak feeling in the back of my knees. "You're looking very grown up, Your Royal Highness," he says. "Will you save a dance for me?"

Will I save a dance for him? It's more likely to be the other way around.

"Of course," I say and smile back at him, even though the light probably reflects off my braces.

Prince Etienne moves on, and I smile politely at more people as they pass in front of us.

My smile turns to a grin when I see the prime minister's family in line. Sophia Orcutt is one of my roommates at the Academie Sainte Marie and my very best friend. I want to rush to her, but protocol means I need to stay where I am.

"Well, Frederick, you've certainly captured a sense of history here tonight," Mr. Orcutt says to my father, a touch of sarcasm in his voice. "Maybe now we can concentrate on the future?"

"I'm always thinking about the future, Francisco," Pap says, giving the prime minister a jovial pat on the shoulder. "One does not happen without the other. Enjoy the evening."

"Indeed." He continues down the line, greeting my mother, then Georgie, and finally nodding politely to me, giving me the barest of glances, which is about what I'd expect from someone as important as the prime minister. Even if I am a princess, most people still think of me as only a kid.

"You look very nice this evening," Mrs. Orcutt says to me, with a slight bob that is almost a curtsy.

I thank her, but it's Sophia I want to talk to. Soon she's in front of me, curtsying. As soon as she stands, I reach out and give her a quick hug, even though that is totally against protocol. She looks so grown up in her long green dress. Her hair, instead of being in braids, is curled and styled and has a ton of hairspray keeping it all in place.

"As soon as we're done here, I'll find you," I say.

"I'll be waiting," she promises.

Then her brother Tobias is bowing to me and Georgie.

My heart does a funny little pitter-pat. Tobias is fifteen and totally cute, with curly blond hair and piercing green eyes. I think I'm a little in love with him, even though he barely talks to me. Tobias doesn't promise to save a dance for me like Etienne did, but I'll make sure I get one at some point. What's the point of being a princess at my first royal ball if I can't dance with the cutest guy in the room?

Finally, the end of the line comes into sight. Soon the fun will start, but before we are allowed to join our friends and dance, Mam and Pap turn to us.

"Remember," Mam says, and I know her remarks are directed at me, because Georgie never has to be told to remember anything. "You represent Colsteinburg tonight, as always. People will be watching everything you do or say. Do not do or say anything you'll regret."

I want to ask my mother if she's never been twelve. I do or say something I regret pretty much hourly. I almost wish I were back in my room with my governess, but I'm not going to miss my chance to finally stay for the whole ball. I wish they would think of me as someone who was important to the country, like Georgie is, instead of someone who constantly has to be watched for inappropriate behavior. I'm growing up. I can see that; why can't they?

"Fritzi could never disappoint us," Pap says. "Go and have fun." He gives me a wink, and I relax.

I hurry to where Sophia and her brother are waiting, as the full orchestra begins the traditional first song, a classical Colsteinburg love song, "*Liebe und Blumen*," featuring strings and horns and timpani. My parents take to the dance floor, gliding across the ballroom in each other's arms. They look so in love it gives me shivers. I want a love like that someday.

"It's like something out of a fairy tale," I say, gripping Sophia's hand. "I can't believe we're both here."

Sophia laughs. "So, which of us is Cinderella?"

I laugh too. "Is one of us a serving girl hoping to meet the prince?"

"Well, I wouldn't mind a dance with Prince Etienne," Sophia admits.

"We just have to watch out when the clock strikes midnight," I joke, though nothing will change for either of us at that magical hour. I'll still be me, Princess Fredericka, and Sophia will still be my best friend.

The king and queen have circled the ballroom three times, and now Georgie and Etienne join them on the dance floor. I see Ivan Frank heading toward me. Mam has arranged to have him partner me for this first dance so I can join them all on the floor. Now, I like Ivan Frank very much, but he's not my idea of an ideal dance partner.

I drop Sophia's hand and grab her brother's. "You must dance with me!"

"Is that a royal directive?" There is a hint of a twinkle in Tobias's eye.

"Yes," I say, grinning. "I'm the princess; you must do as I say."

He bows to me and smiles. "As you wish, Your Royal Highness."

Mr. Frank sees me take to the dance floor and smiles at me, backing away.

We dance, flawlessly, having both attended the same dancing school. I'm aware of eyes on us and pictures being taken. I certainly don't mind being photographed dancing with a cute boy. Tobias even kisses my hand when the dance ends, and my fairy tale is complete.

The ball passes in a rich kaleidoscope of colors and sounds. The orchestra makes the room feel alive with music. It should be easy to save a dance for Etienne, but one government official after another asks me to dance, making me feel very popular, at least with the middle-aged set. Finally, Etienne claims a dance for himself, and it's even more fairy tale-like than dancing with Tobias.

I'm jealous that Georgie gets to dance with him at balls for the rest of her life. She has all the luck.

When we sit down to eat, the array of plates and glasses and utensils is almost baffling even for me, and I'm used to formal meals. The first course features delicately molded Colsteinburg cheese, caviar, and cold cucumber soup. After that's cleared away, there is a salad, featuring, of course, Colsteinburg cheese. We make good cheese here.

"This is sure better than the food at Sainte Marie, isn't it?" Sophia whispers as the main course, filet mignon and a selection of vegetables, is put before us.

"Maybe I can bring leftovers back with me this week, and we can feast!" I answer. Not that the food at school is bad, but it hardly lives up to the dinner at a royal ball.

"Oh, you should," Sophia answers. "Then we can share with Claudia, too." Claudia is our other roommate.

"There will be no leftovers," Tobias says from the other side of me. "Because I plan to eat it all."

We all laugh. It's a night made for laughter.

The dessert is the most amazing of all—red spun-sugar dragons on a white cloud of meringue. It's almost too beautiful to consider eating. Almost.

After dinner, we dance some more. I don't remember a night I've had so much fun.

The orchestra hits the first notes of the Colsteinburg National Anthem, and the dancing stops. I stand by Sophia, our hands on our hearts, as we look toward the white Colsteinburg flag with its red dragon in the center. I have tears in my eyes. It's been such a perfect night, I don't want it to end.

The last notes of the song are still hanging in the air when Mademoiselle Colette appears by my side, looking out of place in her sensible shoes and cardigan.

"It's over, Your Royal Highness."

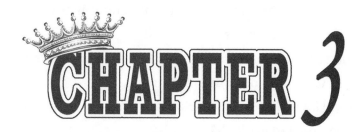

CHAPTER 3

"It is time for bed," Mademoiselle Colette says.

I'm not ready for it to end. Now I understand how awful Cinderella felt when the clock struck midnight. It's like I've been playacting. Monday, I'll be wearing my school uniform again instead of a silk ballgown. I would argue with Mademoiselle Colette, but years of experience have taught me that it's pointless. She always gets her way.

"I'll see you back at school tomorrow night," I say to Sophia and give her a quick hug.

"Yes. See you then." Sophia goes to find her parents. The magic is over for everyone, and I turn back to my governess.

"Did you see me dance with Prince Etienne?" I ask, bouncing on the balls of my feet. "And this dress," I say, twirling to give her the full effect of the silk and lace. "Isn't it the most beautiful dress you ever saw?"

"It's lovely." Mademoiselle Colette reaches for my arm, but I dance just out of her reach.

"Wasn't tonight fantastic beyond belief? I never knew a ball could be this wonderful. I'd always figured it was from what I was allowed to see, but I never knew for sure. Why didn't you tell me how wonderful balls were?"

"Because." Mademoiselle Colette firmly grips my arm so I can't dance away from her again. "You would have been pestering to be included." She leads me out of the ballroom, upstairs, away from the last remnants of the festivities and to my own bedroom.

The heavy velvet curtains are closed, the embroidered bedspread turned down, and my nightgown set out, ready for me to put on, but I'm not ready to get into bed yet.

"This night was just too fabulous!" I spin around the room. Music still plays in my head. My feet won't stay still.

"Let me unzip you, Fredericka," Mademoiselle Colette says, standing patiently in the middle of my room.

I dance my way over to her and let her unzip my dress. It falls in a heap to the floor. I glide to the bed and slip my nightgown over my head. If I close my eyes, it can be a beautiful silk gown instead of sturdy cotton.

"When do you think we'll have another ball?" I ask. "Next week? Next month?" Mam and Pap are always going to balls, whether at our palace or someplace else. Maybe now I can go with them.

"That may be a bit soon," Mademoiselle Colette says as she places my gown on a hanger. "Go brush your teeth."

"I'm not even tired," I say, but I head into the adjoining marble-accented bathroom and wash my face and brush my teeth. As soon as I'm done rinsing, I dance back out.

"Fredericka." Mademoiselle Colette sounds tired, even though I'm not. "Please get in bed. It's after one."

I slide under the covers, but I'll never get to sleep. My feet want to keep dancing. "Good night, Mademoiselle Colette," I say. "I'm going to remember tonight forever."

"Yes, Your Royal Highness," she says softly. "I'm sure you will." She backs out of the room, as if to make sure I don't sneak out of bed before she's gone, then turns out the light and shuts the door.

I stare into the darkness and stretch. Maybe I am a little tired. The best parts of the ball play themselves over and over in my mind, like a highlights video.

I dance and I dance, circling the ballroom floor under the twinkling lights as people chant my name. "Fritzi, Fritzi."

Only family and friends call me Fritzi. Something isn't right.

Mam gently shakes my arm. "Fritzi, wake up."

No. I want to dance some more. I burrow under the covers.

"You have to get up," Mam says. She stops shaking my arm, and her footsteps echo as she walks across the floor. Even from under the blanket, I can tell she's flipped on the light. I peer out just enough to see what time it is. Not even four o'clock.

I push back the covers, rub my eyes, and stare at Mam.

Her hair is pulled back in a ponytail. She's wearing jeans and a sweatshirt and rummaging through my closet.

"What are you doing?"

"You have a backpack someplace here, don't you?"

"*Ja*. I guess." When did I last use it? Maybe our trip to Paris over the summer.

Things are flying out of my closet. Why is she looking for my backpack at four in the morning? Finally, she pulls it out.

"Here," she says, wiping a stray hair from her forehead. "Pack only what is absolutely necessary. Clothes to last a couple of days, and anything you can't live without."

"What?" I rub my eyes again. "Why?"

"There's no time for questions. Just get dressed and pack." She's so sure I'm going to do what she says that she heads out the door.

Outside, there's a crash, and glass shatters. I jump out of bed and push back the curtain. On the other side of the gate, there are people. Dozens of people. Maybe hundreds of people. They're yelling, but I can't tell what they're saying. Some of them have signs, but I can't read them. There are more crashes as the mob throws things over the fence at the palace. Things have obviously progressed beyond letters in the paper. Is this what Mr. Frank was warning Pap about?

I let the curtain drop back into place and run next door to Georgie's room. She's already dressed in jeans and a T-shirt and carefully loading up her own backpack.

"What's going on?" I ask, hands on hips, with maybe just a

little bit of a foot stamp.

Georgie looks up from her packing and frowns. “Why aren’t you dressed yet?”

“There’s a mob out there,” I say. “An angry mob.”

Georgie doesn’t look shocked by that information. “Yes,” she says and puts another pair of pants in her bag. “You better get dressed.”

“Where are we going?”

“Away.” Georgie shoves in another shirt. “We have to hurry.”

“But why?”

Georgie waves her hand at me, as if shooing away an annoying bug.

Fine. I go back to my room and sit on my bed, legs crossed, trying to puzzle this out. Mr. Frank warned of trouble. He said they were looking for the person behind it. But maybe it is too late; maybe the trouble has spread. I jump as something else crashes outside.

Clearly the trouble has spread.

But why? Pap isn’t some crazy tyrannical ruler. He’s nice. He wants what is best for Colsteinburg. Just because some people want different things doesn’t mean they should throw things at us.

What are some of those different things people want? I know I’ve read the letters, seen the complaints and demands, but the only thing that comes to mind is that some people want it to be free to tour the castle, since it technically belongs to the people of Colsteinburg. I remember that because I had visions of tourists wandering in and out of my bedroom all day long.

My door opens, and Georgie bursts in, backpack over her shoulder. "Fritzi! You haven't done a thing!" She opens my drawers and throws jeans and a shirt on the bed. "Put that on."

I do as I'm told while Georgie packs other clothes for me. She scans my room and asks, "Is there anything you must have with you?"

My room is full of souvenirs and favorite things I've collected over the years. There's my dragon collection: everything from whimsical crocheted ones to elegant porcelain ones. There are my snow globes. I have one from every major capital in Europe except Helsinki. I couldn't find one there for some reason. You'd think with all that snow, they'd have lots of snow globes. There are my autographed books and pictures, including one from Prince Harry, which was kind of a joke between us last time we visited England. Sir Fred, my teddy bear, sits up on the shelf, all alone and forgotten. I haven't needed him to sleep with since I was five.

"We're coming back here, aren't we?" I ask.

"I hope so," Georgie answers and shoves my tablet computer and phone into my bag. She grabs some jewelry off my dresser and shoves that in too. Then she zips the bag and hands it to me. "Let's go, Fritzi. We have to leave." She heads out the door without even a look back.

"Wait!" I run after Georgie, my bag thumping against my back.

CHAPTER 4

Only a couple of hours ago, the palace was filled with people and music and laughing and dancing. Now it is eerily quiet, the roar of the crowd outside muted. My breathing sounds too loud in my ears. The hallways are dark, lit only with occasional safety lights near the ground. I stay close to Georgie, as if I've become her very large shadow. She leads me down a back staircase to the service hallways.

When I was little, I used to play down here. It seemed daring to explore in these back rooms and out-of-the-way places and pretend I was a secret agent or a spy. Now it doesn't seem exciting. The whitewashed stone walls and gray doors are cold and scary and sinister. This is not my house; this is not the home I've loved for twelve years. This is some strange and scary place filled with shadows and monsters that might jump out from behind any of those closed doors.

I want to ask what is going on, where everyone is, where Mam and Pap are, but then I see our parents ahead of us in the hall, talking to Marco, the head of palace security. I start to run to them, but Georgie holds me back.

"Just wait," she whispers.

Shortly, Marco salutes and walks away. I break free from Georgie and hurry forward.

"I'll send for you when it's safe, or I'll join you," Pap says to Mam. "Either way, we won't be separated for long."

"Separated!" I cry, rushing to Pap and grabbing his arm as if he's going to vanish right in front of me.

Pap puts his arms around me and holds me tight. "It will only be for a little while, Fritzi."

"Do you promise?" I ask.

Pap looks deep into my eyes. "What have I told you about promises?"

I don't answer. I know what he's going to say. He doesn't make promises, because if something happens, he doesn't want to have to break them.

"My word is enough, right?" he asks.

I nod, my throat feeling thick.

"And I will not make promises that might be impossible to keep."

I nod again.

"But know this. I will do everything in my power to get us together again soon."

"You're king. Everything is in your power."

His smile is so sad it makes me want to cry.

"Maybe not quite everything," he says.

"But why can't you come with us?"

Pap holds me out at arm's length and bends down so he's looking me right in the eye. "I have to stay here. Like you said, I'm the king. If I leave, I'll be giving that up. Abdicating. You don't want that, do you?"

I stare at him in horror. Of course I don't want that.

Georgie clears her throat. "And we're the princesses. During the Blitz in World War Two, Princesses Elizabeth and Margaret stayed in London." She holds her head high.

"I'm glad you know your history, Georgie," Pap says, "but you're not staying."

"I'm not afraid," Georgie says. And I bet she's not. Georgie's not afraid of anything. Except maybe pimples. She freaks out about pimples.

I'm a little bit afraid.

Pap shakes his head. "I'm afraid for you."

"Where are we going?" My voice sounds strange to my ears, too little, too timid, too weak.

"We have friends in America. You will go there."

"When will we come back?" I ask, biting my lower lip. Georgie always tells me to stop doing that. She says it doesn't look elegant.

Right now, I don't care.

Pap's eyes meet mine. "'Though she be but little, she is fierce,'" he says, quoting Shakespeare to me. "That is you, my fierce little Fritzi. I need you to be good and brave. You can do that, right?" he asks. "And soon we'll all be together."

He didn't answer my question, but I don't ask it again. I have a feeling that I wouldn't really like the answer anyway.

Pap looks over his shoulder, like maybe he's expecting the mob to break through at any minute.

"We can't waste time," he says and opens one of the gray doors. There's a van backed up to it with its rear doors open. It looks like the kind of van a kidnapper might use. The kind of thing you see in movies that you know the kid should never get in but does anyway. I'm not getting in that van. I take a step back but bump into Georgie.

"You must hurry," Pap says. He gives me a long hard hug, and I don't ever want him to let go, but he does. Tears are streaming down my face, even though I don't remember starting to cry. Pap helps me into the van. Soon Georgie and Mam are inside too, and the doors slam shut. Pap taps the back door four times as his way of saying a final "*Ich liebe dich*," German for "I love you."

I fall against Georgie as the van drives off, and she puts her arm around me. It's pitch black. There isn't even a window connecting us to the driver's section. I don't know who's driving. I don't know where we're going. I swipe at the tears with the back of my hand, but it doesn't make any difference. More keep falling.

The tires rattle over the gravel drive. The shouts of the protesters are louder but so mixed together I can't make out what they are saying.

Someone bangs on the side of the van, and I jump and squeal. They want in. They want to get us. Why?

"Shh," Georgie says. She's always prepared for every situation, so I'm not surprised when Georgie pulls a little flashlight out of her pocket and shines it around the van. There's a thick, padded blanket in one corner. Georgie snags it and covers us with it as I huddle close to Mam.

Now we are in the dark, in the back of a van, under a blanket. I feel a little safer, even as more people pound on the sides of the van. The van stops, and I try to make myself as small as I can under the blanket. Any minute now, I'm going to throw up, I know it.

"Let me pass," the driver calls out. "I just dropped off a delivery. I got nothing. Let me pass."

The back door rattles as someone tries the handle. I squeak and Mam holds me tight. The van starts moving again, slowly at first, but then with more speed. We're past the mob. We're safe.

Safe in the back of a dark van, fleeing from a mob at the palace. Safe is apparently quite relative.

Georgie pulls the blanket off our heads, and my heartbeat starts to go back to normal. I don't even feel like throwing up anymore.

"What's going on?" I ask.

Mam doesn't answer. Maybe she didn't hear me. Georgie takes my hand in hers. "There are some people causing trouble. It's not safe for us at the palace right now. We're going someplace safe."

"But why all the way to America?" I ask. "Why not just to Switzerland or France?" Those are the countries Colsteinburg is nestled between.

"We need to be farther away from our enemies than that," Georgie says.

Enemies. My stomach does a somersault at that. We have enemies.

"But what about Pap? He isn't safe!"

"He can take care of himself, and it's better if he doesn't have to worry about us," Georgie says.

"I'll miss school." I was only home for the beginning of the Octocentennial, and I'd be expected back at Academie Sainte Marie tomorrow. Today.

"Can't be helped," Georgie says. Mam still says nothing. Maybe she's asleep. Maybe I should sleep. I can't sleep. I'm too wired, too worried.

I've never been this scared before.

I was scared when I first went off to boarding school just last month, but it was more a worry about if I would make friends and like my teachers, not that someone might hurt me.

I was scared the night my grandfather died, a little over a year ago.

We'd been playing Rummy, and after I played the winning

hand, Grandpa put his hand to his heart. I thought he was just surprised I'd won, but then his face twisted up and went gray, and he collapsed, and I screamed for help.

I was pushed aside as medical personnel tried to save King George, but they couldn't. And then Pap was king, and the world was not how it had been before.

The world is changing again.

It's always changing.

I don't like it.

I want to go back to when my great-grandfather was king. Everyone loved King Franz. He was king for more than sixty years. Grandpa had more time to play with me then, and not so many things to stress him out and give him a heart attack. Pap and Mam got dressed up and went out a lot, but they weren't busy all the time either. Things were easier then.

They weren't scary.

They're scary now.

The van's motion is soothing. I curl up and close my eyes, just for a moment.

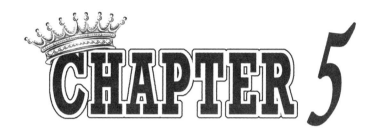

CHAPTER 5

Early morning light splashes across me, and I open my eyes. We've stopped. The back door is open, and Henri, Mam's bodyguard, powerful and reassuring, stands there in a blue deliveryman suit.

"We are here, Your Majesty," he says.

Where is here? My legs quiver as I stand, my muscles protesting against the strange sleeping conditions.

He helps Mam out of the van, and then Georgie, and finally me. There doesn't seem to be any "here" here. There's a brick wall to the left of us, with steel doors at regular intervals. The back of a shopping center, perhaps?

Has Henri betrayed us? Is he going to shoot us or something now that we're in an isolated and remote place? But his face shows a mixture of sadness and sympathy, not the look of someone about to send us to our doom.

There's an old Honda in the otherwise deserted parking area. The door opens, and a tall man steps out. I duck behind Georgie, but no one else seems nervous about this new addition.

In fact, Mam collapses in his arms as he comes closer. For a second, I think it's Pap, joining us after all. But it's not Pap. It's Mr. Frank.

"Cassandra," he says, holding her tight. "Are you okay? Are the girls okay?"

"We're fine, Ivan," Mam says. "Thank you so much for coming. Frederick knew we could count on you."

"Always, my dear Cassandra. But come, we have no time to waste." He lets go of Mam, and she manages to stand on her own. Ivan waves to me and Georgie. "Georgiana, Fredericka, my darling girls. Your carriage awaits."

I grin because this beat-up Honda is about the funniest looking royal carriage I can imagine. Mr. Frank gently touches my cheek as I move past him to the car, and suddenly I want to cry again.

Mr. Frank pulls out of the parking lot, and I want to snuggle up against Georgie, but she's sitting straight and tall and staring out the window. She doesn't look like she wants to comfort me right now. I take a deep breath and look out my window, too.

The sky changes from pearl gray to pale yellow as we drive down mostly empty city streets and then the highway, toward the airport.

"We couldn't have you just climb out of the back of a delivery truck at the airport," Mr. Frank explains. "That would attract too much unwanted attention."

"Why do people want to hurt us?" I ask. Georgie puts her hand on mine and shakes her head. Fine. That's a question for another time. But it's a fair question. I can understand people not liking us—there have always been people who resent royalty—but why do they want to do us harm? We haven't hurt anyone.

"When you get to the airport," Mr. Frank continues, as if I haven't spoken, "go straight to the Monaco Airlines desk. Ask for Lucinda. She's been briefed and will assist you."

Mam nods, and I can tell that Georgie is storing this information away as well.

"You have your diplomatic passports?" he asks.

"We have them," Georgie says, when Mam doesn't seem inclined to answer.

"Okay, good. Keep them safe. But I have a packet for you." He hands a fat manila envelope to Mam, who holds it gingerly, as if expecting it to do something. "Falsified passports and other papers, so that you can function without being noticed. These are what you'll use if asked for I.D. in America." He swivels around in his seat to see Georgie. "Understood?"

Georgie swallows hard and nods. "Right. And where do we go when we get there?"

"There will be a car and driver waiting for you."

"What name will they use?" Georgie asks.

"Cassie Moore," Mr. Frank says and spells out the last name so we understand the difference. "It's the name on the new passport."

Mam is Her Majesty Queen Cassandra Sophia Maria von Boden don Mohr. She is not Cassie Moore. My stomach starts to feel funny again.

We arrive at the airport, and even though it seems like the sun has barely risen, there are cars lined up to discharge passengers and people waiting in security lines.

"Godspeed," Mr. Frank says as he stops the car in front of the main entrance. "I'll let Frederick know you got this far safely."

Mam barely nods. It's Georgie who thanks him and shepherds us out of the car. Ivan Frank drives away, and we're left on the sidewalk, alone.

This is not how we normally arrive at the airport. Every other time we've flown, we've taken a helicopter straight to the tarmac and then boarded our private plane.

No one expects to see the queen and princesses get out of a beat-up Honda, so they don't notice us. I never knew you could be invisible in plain sight before.

"Let's go," Georgie says, taking charge as only Georgie can. She's next in line for the throne, and she will be a great ruler because she really knows how to lead. Now she leads Mam and me through the automatic doors and toward the Monaco Airlines counter.

A man dragging a wheeled carry-on bumps into Mam. She starts to stand tall and regal and put on her true Queen Cassandra look, but he barely gives her a glance, just offers a quick "sorry" and moves on, and she sort of collapses back into herself.

If he knew he'd bumped into the Queen of Colsteinburg, he would have behaved quite differently.

We pass a newsstand, but the headlines are about something that happened in France. No one knows what's happened at the palace yet. What did happen at the palace? Once again, my stomach starts to rebel. Mam and Georgie are getting ahead of me. I hurry to catch up.

At the Monaco Airlines counter, it's Georgie who does all the talking, while Mam looks on.

"We were told to speak to Lucinda," Georgie says.

"I'm sure I can help you," the young man at the counter says. I know what that's all about. Like all guys who come in contact with Georgie and her blond hair and startling blue eyes, he's instantly in love and doesn't want to miss a chance to talk to her.

"You can help us by finding Lucinda so we can speak to her. It's very important," Georgie says. She manages to be firm and flirt at the same time. I'll have to get her to teach me how to do that.

Within moments, an older woman—with a short, no-nonsense haircut, glasses perched on the end of her nose, and a name tag that says "Lucinda"—appears at the counter. Georgie looks to Mam to take over, but she doesn't seem inclined to speak up. Mam acts like she's sleepwalking or in a daze.

"My name is Georgiana," Georgie says, softly but clearly. "Ivan

Frank told me to speak to you."

The woman's eyes light up with recognition. It's the first time we've been recognized since we got into the airport, but she clearly realizes that she shouldn't say anything. "Yes, of course. Please, follow me."

She leads us through a door behind the counter, and we make our way through the private passageways of the airport.

"I'm so sorry, Your Majesty," Lucinda says. "This is a terrible turn of events."

Mam responds to the title and nods. "Thank you," she says. "We are hopeful things will right themselves soon."

Yes, that's what I want to hear. Things will be better soon, and we won't have anything to worry about. Everyone is just being overly cautious. This is a little vacation. That's all.

We bypass all the security lines and ticket counters and board the plane before everyone else.

"The seats up there look much nicer," I say as I try to get comfortable in my narrow one.

"We're not flying first class," Georgie says. "We're regular tourists today."

Regular tourists who boarded the plane even before the flight crew. When the flight crew does come on board, the pilot introduces himself to Mam and tells her he's honored to have her on his plane. That is the only recognition we get.

After we take off, Mam buries herself in a magazine. Georgie takes out a calculus book and starts working problems. Only

Georgie would think to bring a calculus book with her. Doing math problems calms her down, so it makes sense. I take out my phone and shove the bag under my seat. Earbuds in place, I lean back and fall asleep.

Mam nudges me awake when they bring food around, but I'm not hungry and wave them away. I sleep some more. I don't have to think while I'm sleeping.

I wake up when they announce we are getting ready to land.

The plane lands at Boston's Logan International Airport, and there is no more special treatment. We have to wait with the crowds of other people trooping off the plane, down the passenger boarding bridge, and into the terminal. We don't have to stop for luggage, though, so we get to customs and immigration before the crowd.

Georgie pulls out our new passports and shows them to the guy in the glass booth. He barely glances at them before handing them back and waving us through.

And then reality hits in the shape of a sign saying "Moore," with Mam acknowledging that she is Cassie Moore. Just plain Cassie Moore, not Her Majesty Queen Cassandra Sophia Maria von Boden don Mohr.

If Mam's not queen anymore, am I still a princess?

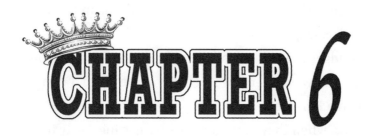

CHAPTER 6

A couple of years ago, we flew to New York City and stayed in the penthouse suite on the top floor of a Fifth Avenue hotel. We could look out the windows and see the whole world, or at least that's what it felt like. We went to the top of the Empire State Building and the Statue of Liberty and had front row seats at a Broadway show.

This is not New York.

I look out the car windows and don't see the massive, powerful buildings that define New York. Boston is smaller, more approachable. But even without the huge buildings, the crush of cars on the highway makes me long for open spaces. The car enters a tunnel, and my heart feels squeezed in my chest. I'm not claustrophobic. I've been in tunnels before, but today I don't want to be underground surrounded by walls. It reminds me too much of being in the back of the dark van. I reach for Georgie's hand, and she gives mine a reassuring squeeze. When we emerge, there is still more traffic, with no one behaving in an orderly way. It's almost like driving in Rome or Paris. Are drivers everywhere crazy?

Ahead of us, an amazing suspension bridge rises geometrically above the horizon. I want to go over it and see what it looks like up close, but we turn, and it recedes in the distance. We drive beside the river, the city on the other side of us. We pass an amphitheater that looks like a massive shell. It's all too much to take in. I want my familiar scenery: mountains and fields and red tile roofs. I want to be home.

We cross the river. I want to ask where we are going but suppose the answer won't really matter. Other than that we landed in a city called Boston, I have no idea where we are or what might possibly be around here. We exit the highway and drive on crowded city streets and finally to an area where there is not as much traffic and things seem slightly more spread out. The car pulls up in front of a two-story building with several entrances.

The door on the end opens up. A tall slender man, with his dark hair cropped in what I always think of as a military style, comes out and helps Mam out of the car.

"Cassandra," he says, his voice smooth and warm. "I'm glad you made it here safely."

Mam grips his hand with her own, her knuckles white. "Thank

you, Thomas." The shakiness of her voice makes my insides tighten up. I want to go home.

"It's good to see you, girls," the man says. "Come inside where we can talk."

"Who is he?" I whisper to Georgie as we follow him and Mam into the house.

"Ambassador Hart," she says matter-of-factly. "You remember him? He was the ambassador to Colsteinburg a few years ago. Remember his wife used to wear really high heels, and we always wondered how she didn't topple over?"

That is vaguely familiar.

"They have a son, Matthew, remember him? He's a few years older than I am."

"Kind of," I say, but I don't really. I have a vague image of a tall skinny kid with glasses who didn't pay any attention to me. "Why is he here?"

"He owns the house," Georgie answers, and we step over the threshold and inside.

Ambassador Hart closes the door behind us. We are in a small living room. There is a sofa and two easy chairs and a TV. Behind that, I can see a dining room and a kitchen. That seems to be all there is to the downstairs.

"You live here?" I ask. If he and his family live here, in this small house, where on earth were Mam and Georgie and I going to sleep?

"No," he answers. "We bought this place when my son was in

college. Now that he's graduated, we were getting it ready to sell. I'm honored to be able to offer it for your use for the time being."

"Oh," I answer rather ungraciously. I toss my backpack on the floor and flop down in one of the chairs. It squeaks as I settle into it.

"Thank you, it is very generous of you," Georgie says when it becomes clear Mam isn't planning on responding. She sits next to Mam, who is on the sofa running her fingers over the edging of a throw pillow, staring out at nothing. I can't look at Mam; it scares me.

"I'm glad I can help," he says. "I wish I could do more."

So do I, but I don't say anything.

Ambassador Hart sits in the other chair and addresses Mam and Georgie. "I didn't have a lot of time to get things ready. The beds are made up, and there are towels in the linen closet. I stopped at the store on my way here and picked up some staples for you. There are take-out menus on the counter and some cash as well."

"What's going to happen next?" Georgie asks, her voice surprisingly strong, considering everyone else seems to be falling apart.

"I don't know for certain," Ambassador Hart admits. "The key now is to keep you all safe and secluded."

"Until Pap fixes everything and sends for us, right?" I ask. That has to be the right answer.

"That would be ideal, yes," he says slowly, leading me to believe he doesn't really think that's going to happen. My insides twist into a knot. "It's really too soon to know exactly what will happen. For now, the main thing is to keep you all safe."

"Will anyone know we're here?" Georgie asks.

"Only my wife and I."

"Are we allowed to leave the house?" I ask, feeling fretful. I don't want to be a prisoner.

"With caution, I'd say yes, after a couple of days."

"How will we shop?" Georgie asks.

"Between what I've brought today and the money for takeout you should be fine for several days. When you need more, there is a corner store about two blocks away. It's an easy walk, and you should be able to get what you need there. This is only temporary until Frederick comes for you or until we can come up with a more permanent solution."

The only permanent solution I want to see is us going back home to Pap.

"My number is on the counter. If you need anything, call."

"What about security?" Georgie asks. We're the royal family, we never go anywhere without security.

Ambassador Hart shakes his head slowly. "I'm sorry. I can't do anything for you there. I spoke with the State Department. They don't want to appear to be taking sides in this conflict."

"Taking sides?" I say. "But I thought the United States were our friends. I thought you would help us."

"We are friends of the country of Colsteinburg," he says. "That does not mean we are partial to any particular administration."

I glower at him, but it doesn't seem to affect him in any way.

"So we're on our own," Georgie says.

Mr. Hart runs his hand through his cropped hair. "You are here because I, personally, chose to offer you help. It is a strictly private matter. The government will not get involved. But you do have whatever help I can give you."

"Why can't we just go home?" I ask.

"You have to be reasonable, Fredericka," he says. "Your country is in chaos. The safest place for you is here."

Personally, I think we'd be safer somewhere with security, but no one will listen to me. I'm just a kid.

"I have to go." Ambassador Hart stands. "I'm sorry, but I need to catch my plane back to DC. I have a dinner party tonight, and I don't want to raise questions about where I've been."

"Thank you," Georgie says again, also standing. Mam and I don't move. "We really do appreciate all you are doing for us."

"Goodbye, Cassandra, girls," he says. "I'll be in touch. Good luck."

He leaves, and we are alone in our new home. No. Not home. Temporary shelter. A new kind of hotel. That's all.

"I'll put on tea, Mam," Georgie says. "Does that sound good?"

Mam nods absently, still running her fingers over the edge of the pillow.

Georgie heads to the kitchen, and I jump up from my chair and follow her. She fills the kettle at the tap and puts it on the stove, studying the knobs to see how to turn it on. Finally, she gets the burner lit. She locates a box of teabags and puts them on the counter.

"Do you want tea, too?"

"I don't know." I open the refrigerator and see that there are several cans of soda in there. "I'd rather have a soda."

"Fine," Georgie says. She puts teabags in two mugs and leans against the counter, waiting for the water to boil.

I grab a can of soda and head upstairs to investigate the rest of the house. There are two bedrooms, one with a very large bed and one with a double bed. That's it. Mam will obviously have the big room with the big bed, but that means Georgie and I will have to share the smaller room. I can't sleep with anyone else in bed with me.

This stinks. I sit on the edge of the double bed, sip my soda, and close my eyes. This is only temporary. Soon Pap will get everything straightened out at home, and we'll be back at the palace.

I take a deep breath. Grandpa always said a person can deal with anything for a short time. Besides, it's not like school is so luxurious. The beds are narrow and not so soft, and I share a room with two other girls.

Sophia and Claudia!

I need to get in touch with them. They're going to be so worried when I don't show back up at school tonight. If they hear about what happened at the palace, they might think I'm hurt or even dead. I need to let them know I'm okay.

Leaving my soda on the dresser, I fly down the stairs to where my backpack and phone are.

"Fritzi, really," Mam says as I hurtle into the living room. "You sound like a herd of elephants."

I rummage around in my bag for the phone I know is there. "I need to message Sophia and Claudia," I say. "I have to tell them where I am."

"No!"

I drop my bag and stare at Mam. "Why? I need to let them know I'm not dead or something."

"You can't," she says.

"But they're going to worry when I don't show up at school."

What will they think when they hear about what happened? Will they hear? Is what happened at home on the news? I glance at the TV, but maybe this isn't the best time to turn it on and check.

"You can't tell people where we are," Georgie says, coming in from the kitchen.

"Not even Sophia?"

"No."

"What about Madame Colette? Does she know? She'll be worried."

"No one," Georgie says. "We're hiding."

Hiding?

The word hits me as if someone just punched me in the stomach. "But surely we're not hiding from Sophia or Claudia or

Mademoiselle Colette."

"From everyone," Georgie answers firmly.

"But why?" I'm not sure I want to know the answer. If we are hiding from everyone, then we really are in danger. Not just danger if we stay in the palace, but danger no matter where we are. And we have no security. How are we supposed to stay safe with no security? And no one can know where we are, except the Harts. Are the Harts more trustworthy than Mademoiselle Colette or Sophia? How can we be sure?

"It's complicated," Georgie says, in that ever so condescending way that they must teach big sisters. "But it's safer for all of us if no one knows where we are. And that means no social media either. Radio silence. Got it?"

I want to run. To get out. To escape all this craziness. I glance toward the door, but where would I go? I don't know where I am and wouldn't know how to get back. Who are we hiding from? Could they be out there somewhere, waiting for us? I head up the stairs two at a time and slam the door of the little bedroom behind me before flopping onto the bed and letting myself cry.

It takes about fifteen minutes before Georgie comes up and sits on the bed next to me. She places her hand gently on my back, a soothing gesture that I'm more used to receiving from Mam or Pap.

"You have to be strong," she says.

I sit up and wipe my eyes. "I don't understand what happened. Yesterday there was the ball. Today we're hiding."

Georgie takes a deep breath. “I can’t say I understand it all either, but this is what I do know. There is an effort to overthrow Pap. People may get violent. Pap wants us out of the way and out of danger. That’s why we can’t say where we are.”

“Is Pap still king?” I ask.

“He is,” Georgie answers, but she sounds a little unsure.

“He’s going to stay king, right?” It’s impossible to think of our family not ruling Colsteinburg. It’s our country, we founded it. My great-grandfather was king for more than sixty years. We are Colsteinburg.

“I hope so,” Georgie says, and there is a faraway look in her eye. She’s the next in line for the throne. If Pap isn’t king, then she may never get to be queen. That’s not really fair to her; she doesn’t even get a say in it. Georgie lets out a deep breath and returns from wherever her thoughts have taken her. “Listen. I’m worried about Mam.”

I slump down, all the strength going out of me. “What’s wrong with her?” Since when does Mam not take charge? She is the queen: the always dignified Queen Cassandra. But now she seems to have disappeared inside of herself.

“I don’t know,” Georgie says, “but we’re going to have to take care of her until we can be with Pap again.” She stands up and walks to the window, pushing aside the plastic mini-blinds, and peers outside.

I hug the pillow to me, wishing I’d brought my teddy bear with me. “I want it to be yesterday again,” I say. “Before the ball.

Before everything went wrong!"

Georgie turns to me with a sad grin. "So, do I, Fritzi. Oh, so do I."

She comes to the bed and hugs me, and I hang on tight. I'm afraid to let go. What if she's all I have left?

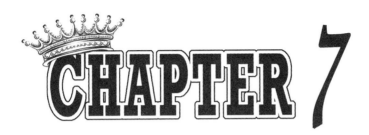

CHAPTER 7

A day has never passed so slowly. There is nothing to do. Nowhere to go. No one to see. Mam sits on the sofa in the living room, drinking tea when Georgie brings it to her. We put a frozen lasagna in the oven for our dinner. When it is barely dark out, we climb into bed.

Mam takes the small room, leaving the larger bed for me and Georgie. We lie side by side in the near-darkness and don't say a word. I can tell her I'm scared, but she knows that. There's no point in repeating the same thing over and over.

Monday and Tuesday pass in much the same way. We all nap most of the day, which Georgie says is due to jet lag. Maybe. Or maybe we can't think of anything better to do.

By Wednesday, I wish we'd stayed in Colsteinburg. At least

being in danger wouldn't be boring.

I go downstairs after yet one more nap. I haven't slept this much since I was a baby, and yet I'm still always tired. Mam is watching TV, a cup of coffee cooling on the table in front of her. She doesn't look up, and I go into the kitchen, where Georgie is sitting at the table, an open can of soda in front of her. "I put the last frozen dinner in the oven," she says, and I can smell the delicious aroma of tomatoes and spices coming from the oven. "I guess tomorrow we're going to have to learn to cook or start getting take out."

"Do you know how to cook?"

Georgie sighs. "Someone's going to have to figure it out."

"Mam?"

The look Georgie gives me lets me know that was a dumb question.

"Then we'll get takeout."

"I don't know how long the money Mr. Hart gave us will have to last," Georgie says.

I sit down on one of the vinyl-covered kitchen chairs. "We have our own money."

"Only what we brought with us. And we'd have to change it to dollars."

"Credit cards?" I ask, hopefully.

"I don't know," Georgie says. "I'm not sure we'll have the money to pay them off until things settle down, or even if they still work."

"We'll starve!" I say, my stomach already starting to grumble in anticipation.

"No." Georgie gets up and peers into the other room, but Mam is still staring at the TV. Georgie comes back and then sits down with me. She twists an emerald ring on her finger. "And if I have to, I can sell this, or pawn it or something."

"You can't! You got it from Etienne!"

Georgie stares at the shimmering green stone. "It's just a ring. And if it's between this and starving ..."

Not that I'd rather starve, but still. "But Etienne. He gave it to you almost like an engagement ring. How can you get rid of it?"

"If everything works out all right, we'll buy a new ring. And if it doesn't ..." Georgie's eyes have a sadness in them I don't remember ever seeing before. "Well, then the fewer reminders the better."

If we don't get the kingdom back, the official arrangement that Georgie marry Etienne would probably be called off.

"You can still marry him, you know," I say. "Nothing would stop you."

"You don't think so?" Georgie says, a touch of bitterness in her voice. "I think you're living in a dream world."

Maybe. But my dream world is a happier place. I like it there.

I twist the dragon ring I wear on my pinkie finger. "If we need to sell rings, we'll start with this one," I say.

"Hopefully it won't come to that," Georgie says and takes a deep breath. "I found out some stuff about home today," she says.

"And?" I ask, almost afraid to breathe while I wait for her

answer. We checked, Georgie and I, every few hours when we were actually awake, for some news that was actually news and would tell us something useful. So far there's been nothing.

Georgie takes me by the hand and leads me upstairs to our room. "It's better to talk about these things away from Mam."

I don't like that. I want Mam to be in charge. I don't want to have to protect her from things. She's supposed to be protecting us.

Georgie turns on her tablet computer.

"What did you find out?" I ask. I don't want to wait for her to show me some web page. I want her to tell me everything is going to be okay. That's the only answer I'm really looking for here.

"It's Sophia's father."

"What?" That answer doesn't even make sense.

"He's behind it all," Georgie says flatly.

"No, he's not. He's the prime minister. He's one of Pap's friends."

"He's the prime minister, it's true," Georgie answers, "but I'm not sure how much of a friend he is." She pulls up a website that shows the palace of Colsteinburg, our beloved home, with the universal symbol for no, a red circle and slash, superimposed over it.

Instead of the familiar white flag with red dragon, the page shows a flag with green and white stripes and a strange four-pointed star in the middle that looks like something from outer space.

"What's that supposed to mean?" I ask, pointing at the picture and trying to push back the sick feeling in my stomach.

"They want Colsteinburg to be a modern country," she says.

"We're modern!" I protest. "We have electricity and toilets and cars and internet. What more do they want?"

"They want a modern government, not a monarchy."

"Britain has a monarchy, no one says they're not modern. And Denmark and Belgium and Monaco." This isn't fair. We had to flee from our home because someone wants what we already have?

"They want a democracy," Georgie says. There is a strain in her voice, and I can tell I'm testing her patience.

"Democracy is not modern." I learned about this from my tutor. "The Greeks had a democracy thousands of years ago."

"Fritzi, you don't have to convince me," Georgie says. "We're on the same side, remember?"

I take a deep breath and fight back tears. "Right." I flop down on the bed next to her, burying my face in the comforter. After a minute, I roll over and ask, "So, what do we do? How do we fix this?"

"We don't," Georgie says. "We can't fix this. We have to let things play out."

"Why?" I ask. "Mr. Orcutt is not letting things play out. He's actively doing something. We should actively resist."

"That's for Pap to do, not us."

Arguing probably isn't going to get me anywhere, but I'm not sure I agree. If we can be the face of Colsteinburg at events big and small, why can't we speak up for it when it's in trouble?

"Why now?" I ask. "Why during the Octocentennial? Why take a time when everyone is celebrating the history of the country to say you want to change everything?"

"Precisely because it is the Octocentennial," Georgie says. "He's saying that a twenty-first century country doesn't need a government formed in the middle ages."

"So, he wants to be president or something?"

"He says there should be an election, but yes, he wants to be president or something."

I swipe at my wet eyes with the back of my hand and sit up. "Why doesn't Pap just run for president too? Then Orcutt would see that people really do like Pap."

Georgie leaves her tablet on the bed and walks over to the window. She stares off into the distance. "I'm not sure people really do like Pap. They liked King Franz, but ..."

"Not like Pap?" I jump off the bed and turn on her. "Everyone likes Pap. He's the nicest guy in the world. He's smart and funny and sweet and handsome. What is there not to like?"

"Fritzi," Georgie says, keeping her voice calm and soothing.

"Don't 'Fritzi' me," I say. "Okay, maybe Pap isn't as good at being king yet as King Franz was, but King Franz was king for more than sixty years. Pap just needs to get used to it. Mr. Orcutt needs to give him time."

"It doesn't work like that, Fritzi," Georgie says.

"It should," I say.

Francisco Orcutt needs to be convinced to be patient. And who could convince him? His daughter, Sophia, of course.

I can text Sophia, and we can work this out between us. Maybe having Francisco Orcutt be in charge of the opposition is a good thing; I can actually do something now.

I pull out my phone, and before Georgie can ask what I'm doing, I type, *We need to talk. We need to make our fathers see reason and compromise. Are you with me?*

The second I hit send, the doorbell rings.

We stare at each other as if this simple, homey sound is the start of a grand invasion. I'm almost afraid to breathe as we hurry downstairs. Mam is staring at the door, her eyes wide, her hands gripping a throw pillow.

Georgie stands up straighter and heads to the door, wearing her courage like a cape. She looks through the peephole and then throws the door open.

Standing on our front step is Henri.

Mam jumps up. "Henri! Did you bring Frederick? Is Frederick here?" She rushes to him. He steps inside and closes the door. He is alone.

"I'm sorry, Your Majesty," he says. "The king is not with me."

Mam sinks back onto the sofa. "Is he safe?"

"He was safe and healthy when I left him," Henri says. "He wants very much to be with all of you, but he must stay and fight for the kingdom."

"What is he doing to fight for the kingdom?" I ask. "How is he fighting? Can we help?"

"Ah." Henri smiles at me and gives a slight bow in my direction. "Your Royal Highness, your desire to help is admirable, but what you can do right now is stay here and safe so your father does not have to worry about you."

It doesn't seem like nearly enough.

Then I remember the text I sent Sophia. I am doing something to help.

Sophia and I will save the kingdom.

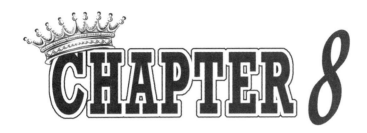

CHAPTER 8

We share dinner with Henri, and when we are done, and Mam and Henri have coffee in front of them, he says, "I'm afraid you may be here longer than we anticipated."

"Longer?" Georgie asks, a strain in her voice.

"How long?" I demand. "We only brought a few clothes with us. We don't have enough to stay longer. And what about school? I'm missing school. I can't miss school!" My voice is rising to a level of near-hysteria, and there's nothing I can do to stop it. "Education is important! You keep telling me that!" I yell at Mam. "And how am I supposed to learn anything stuck in this stupid little condo? If we can't go home, I should at least be allowed to go to school!"

I push back from the table and run upstairs, not caring if I sound like—as Mam would say—"a herd of elephants." I slam the door and throw myself on the bed. It's not fair. It's just not fair. If only we had stayed home, then we could help. Here we do nothing. I hate doing nothing. The tears run down my cheeks, and I don't even try to rub them away. What's the point?

If Sophia would at least get in touch with me, then maybe I could do something.

I hate feeling so helpless. So powerless.

I mean, I'm twelve; I've never really wielded much power, I suppose, but I've never felt helpless like this.

There is a soft knock at the door, and without waiting for an answer (which I wasn't inclined to give anyway), Georgie comes in. She sits next to me on the bed. "Well, it looks like you're going to get what you want," she says.

I sit up, feeling a hundred times better. "I'm going back to Academie Sainte Marie?" I can't wait to see Sophia and Claudia again. And to have things to do. Even Monsieur Garçon's grammar class, as boring as it is, will be better than sitting around here staring at the walls. "And it's safe there," I continue, wiping the remains of the tears from my face. "They are really careful about who gets into the buildings. No one could bother me there. When do I leave? Will Henri fly over with me? Is that why he came?"

Georgie doesn't answer right away, and when I finally look at her, she is slowly shaking her head. She doesn't look nearly as happy as I feel.

"What?" I ask, not at all certain I want to know the answer.

"You're not going to Academie Sainte Marie."

"But—" I can't even think what she might mean. "You said I was going to school."

"Yes. The local middle school," she says.

I stare at her. "The what?" Panic snakes its way through all my internal organs. "But how is that safe? If we are hiding? How is that going to work?"

"Come down and talk to Henri," she says.

"I don't want to," I say.

"You're the one who said you should go to school," Georgie points out.

"I meant to Academie Sainte Marie."

"You can see if you can convince him of that," Georgie says in a tone I know means she thinks I have no hope of succeeding. "At least going out to school every day won't be as boring as sitting around here."

She kind of has a point about that.

"Okay, I'll talk to him."

It turns out Mam is completely against the idea.

"It's not safe," she keeps repeating. "She needs to stay here with me where we can keep her safe."

Suddenly going to the local school sounds like a great option.

"I'm sure people don't just wander in off the street into the schools. There is security," I say.

"Certainly," Henri says. "She would be safe in a school. And no one would have any reason to think that Princess Fredericka is there. We would enroll her under the name on the falsified passport. It is probably better for her to be in school anyway. School attendance is compulsory up until age sixteen. If she is seen here, someone could report her as truant. You don't want the investigation that would come with that."

Mam looks trapped and finally folds back in on herself. "Do whatever you think is best."

So, the next morning, quite as a matter of course, Henri drives me over to the middle school in his rented car, with Georgie along for moral support. Mam refuses to leave the condo, locking herself in her bedroom before we've even left.

The school office is light and airy. On one side of a long counter, secretaries are busy typing and answering phones. We wait on the other side for a guidance counselor to see me and give me a schedule. We've already presented all sorts of cobbled together documents that say I'm Fritzi Moore and live in town. A girl with ripped jeans and pink stripes in her black hair drops a paper off in the overflowing "In" basket. She looks me up and down and, with a wrinkle of her nose, leaves, thinking she has me all figured out. But she doesn't know me at all. I may be in jeans and a wrinkled T-shirt, but I am a princess, and she is just a girl with pink hair.

A moment later, a short, round woman comes in. "And

what have we here?" she asks with that false cheeriness people sometimes use when talking to children. "A new student? How lovely."

"This is Fritzi Moore," the secretary says. "She's starting today and needs a schedule."

Fritzi Moore is not my name, but it's the one on the false passport, and Georgie points out that I needed a name I would answer to. The thing is, Fredericka Elisabetta Teresa von Boden don Mohr sounds regal and impressive. Fritzi Moore sounds like a snack.

"What grade are you in, Trixie?"

"Fritzi," I correct, and then start to answer "fifth class" but realize that's not right. It's not what we figured out last night reading up on the school system in the United States. "Seventh grade," I say, but it feels so wrong.

"And what was the name of your old school?"

"Academie Sainte Marie," I answer without thinking. She quirks an eyebrow at me. "It's in France."

Georgie kicks me in the shin, and Henri frowns at me. Oh, right, I probably shouldn't have told her that much.

"Do you speak English?" the woman asks, speaking slowly and with exaggerated enunciation.

Aren't I speaking English with her right now? "*Oui*," I say, and Georgie kicks me again. I mentally stick my tongue out at her and continue. "I'm fluent in English, German, and French."

"We have a place in a Spanish class for you," she says.

"I speak English, German, and French," I repeat, slower.

"Exactly why you should learn Spanish."

Actually, I can't fault her logic.

"Let's go next door to my office," the woman says, "and leave your parents to fill out the emergency forms."

I look at Georgie in shock, but she just shrugs. She's only six years older than me. How anyone could possibly think she is my mother is beyond me. And Henri, as father? Well, he at least is the right age, and if we aren't telling them who my real parents are, why shouldn't they think what they will?

I follow the counselor to her office, which is approximately the size of my closet back home. She squeezes behind the desk and indicates I should sit in one of the two guest chairs.

She starts typing on her computer, and a few minutes later, she hands me a schedule. Spanish, math, phys. ed., English, geography, science, and cooking.

"Can't I take German or French?"

"We don't offer German, and what's the point of taking a beginner French class if you are fluent already?"

I should have kept quiet about being fluent. Then I could have taken an easy class. I wouldn't mind sleeping through beginner French. But then again, if I learn Spanish, I can show off to my friends back at Academie Sainte Marie that I know another language. If I go back to Academie Sainte Marie. My shoulders sag a little. I want my old life back.

By the time we get back to the office, Henri has finished filling out the paperwork, and Georgie grabs me by the hands. "Good luck," she says. "We'll be back at three to pick you up."

I swallow hard. I want this. Kind of. But I don't want her to leave. "*Danke*," I whisper.

Georgie and Henri head out the door, and the guidance counselor says, "I'll show you to your locker and your first class. Don't worry, Lizzie, you'll get along just fine here."

"Fritzi," I say through clenched teeth.

She leads me down a hallway lined with green lockers until she reaches number 791. "Do you have a lock?"

"What for?"

She frowns. "Be sure to bring one in tomorrow. It's better not to leave anything in your locker until you do."

Great, so they've abandoned me at a school full of thieves. I'm going to get them for this.

CHAPTER 9

Each closed door we pass has a window, and I can see students sitting at desks, gathering around computers, scribbling in notebooks; teachers are writing on whiteboards, walking around classrooms, lecturing.

It's just like Sainte Marie's except the building isn't two hundred years old, and the girls aren't all wearing matching scratchy wool skirts.

The guidance counselor opens one of the doors and signals to the teacher, a young woman in a skinny skirt and high heels. She reminds me of the new press secretary back at the castle.

"Señora Sanchez," the counselor says, "this is Bitzy Moore. She'll be in your class."

"Fritzi," I say.

"Nice to have you, Fritzi," Señora Sanchez says and smiles.

I stare at all the people staring at me. The girl with the pink hair smirks and turns to the girl next to her. "Frizzy! Ha! What an appropriate name!"

A couple of people laugh, and I glare at Pinkie. I resist the urge to reach up and touch my hair. I know it's safely tucked into its braid.

"Would you like to introduce yourself to the class, Fritzi?" Señora Sanchez asks.

I stand tall and nod. They'll stop laughing when I tell them I'm a princess. But as I open my mouth to speak, I remember I can't say a word. I can't tell them that I'm Her Royal Highness, Princess Fredericka Elisabetta Teresa von Boden don Mohr of Colsteinburg.

I take a deep breath and say, "I'm Fritzi Moore." Rows of staring eyes watch me. "We just moved here. From France." Which would explain the French school, if anyone cared to check, and my unusual accent. I slip into a seat in the front row.

Señora Sanchez hands me a book from the shelf. "You'll want to get that covered tonight," she says, and I pretend I know what she's talking about. Then she continues the class as if there was no interruption.

I open Georgie's calculus notebook, the only notebook we had on hand, and carefully copy the notes the teacher writes on the board. It's all about conjugating verbs and gender in nouns. I can do this stuff in my sleep.

An electronic tone sounds, and there's a scramble as everyone puts away their notebooks and stands up.

"What class do you have next?" a girl in faded jeans and a pink polo shirt asks.

"Math," I say and hand over my schedule.

She scans it before handing it back. "We're in all the same classes. So I can help get you situated. I'm Bethany." She heads out of the classroom, and I follow. "So, you're French?" she asks, letting me catch up with her in the hall.

"No." I wish I could tell her the truth. I want to tell everyone the truth. "I went to school in France, but I'm not French."

"So, what are you?" she asks.

Instead of lying, I ask a question of my own. "I'm a little nervous, a new school and all. Are people nice here?"

"Most of them," she says. "Stay away from Jasmine, though. She thinks she's a real princess."

Hmmm. I wonder which one is Jasmine.

"So, what kind of name is Fritzi? I don't think I've ever heard it before. It's cute."

"It's a nickname." It's all I can say without giving more away.

"What's it short for?" Bethany persists as we head toward the staircase.

I didn't realize I'd have to have a whole secret history figured out before going to math. I can't tell her it's a nickname for Fredericka and also in honor of my great-great-great grandfather King Fritz, no matter how much I might want to.

Someone bumps me from behind, and I spin around to see Pinkie smirking at me. "Oh look, it's Frizzy."

There are a thousand comebacks on the tip of my tongue, but unfortunately most of them aren't in English. Before I can translate them in my mind, she and her cabal of giggling friends have run off.

I'm nearly exploding with unspoken retorts. Bethany, who didn't speak up for me in any language, says, "Ignore her. Jasmine thinks she's so cool, but she's just a big jerk."

So, that's Jasmine, is it? I'm seething. I've seen girls get picked on before, and I always speak up for them, but it's never been me being picked on. No one makes fun of a princess. At least not to her face. I don't like it.

Jasmine may think she's a princess, but I'll have to show her how a real princess behaves. Trust me, I've had plenty of instruction.

Bethany leads me up the stairs and into a classroom that is nearly identical to the one downstairs. She heads to a desk in the front, and I look around for a possible empty seat, maybe in the back, where I can be invisible, but Bethany waves me over to where she is talking to a boy and a girl.

"Fritzi, this is Miles"—she points to a guy with ears that are a little too big for his head and glasses that keep sliding down his nose—"and Kim"—who is several inches shorter than I am and wears her black hair in pigtails. She looks about ten. "Fritzi is new here, and I figured I'd make sure she got off to a good start by meeting the right people."

The right people? I glance around the classroom to the other kids, who are finding their seats. Girls who look like models, boys with a devil-may-care attitude. What makes some people the right people and some not?

If people don't know I'm a princess, will they still think I'm one of the "right" people to know? I only have the clothes Georgie packed for me so quickly the other day. My hair straightener and all the things I use to make myself look a little less like a dork each morning were left behind. They'll simply think of me as the new kid with braces, a thick red braid, and a wrinkled T-shirt. I wish I could tell them I'm a princess. I slide into an empty seat as the teacher comes into the room.

He starts lecturing before the door even clicks shut. I scramble to get out my notebook and try to keep up. Halfway through class, he notices me and asks who I am. He hands me a book and goes right back to his lecture. A very intense teacher.

When class ends, I look toward some of the beautiful people, but they don't notice me. Bethany, however, is right over my desk again, ready to guide me to my next class.

The next class is gym, where I find I'm expected to have shorts, a T-shirt, and sneakers to change into each day. Since I don't have the appropriate clothes today, I sit on the bleachers and watch the class.

They break up into teams to play basketball. Finally, it's a chance to observe without anyone expecting anything of me.

I can see that Bethany and her friends, while friendly, are not terribly competent at this game. Frankly, it doesn't even look like they're trying.

The girl with the pink hair, on the other hand, whom I might expect to be a prima donna afraid of chipping her nail polish, is actually quite good.

I haven't played basketball, but I have played netball, which is similar. Pinkie may be a jerk, but we might have more in common than I have with Bethany and her friends.

After gym class, Bethany escorts me to the cafeteria for lunch. She and her friends get in line to buy food, and I look for a place to sit with the bag lunch Georgie packed for me. A large round table by the window is bright and sunny and empty. I pick the sunniest spot and sit down.

"You can't sit there," a girl at the next table tells me, her voice low, as if giving me some dire warning.

"Of course I can," I say and take my sandwich out of my bag.

"You're new here; you don't understand," the girl says. "That's Jasmine's table."

Of course it is. I open my water and allow a smile to spread across my face. Jasmine's going to have to get used to the fact that Princess Fredericka is here now.

Conversations at the surrounding tables die away, and a shadow falls over me. I look up to see pink-haired Jasmine holding her tray and glaring at me.

"That's my seat, Frizzy," she says.

It would be so simple to answer with something like "I don't see your name on it." But that would sound juvenile and not worthy of a princess. "There are plenty of seats at this table." I take a sip of my water.

"You can't sit here," Jasmine says again, still standing there with her tray.

"And yet, I am."

Jasmine taps her foot. "You're going to have to move."

"No, really, I'm not." This is getting annoying.

Bethany swoops in like an avenging angel. "Fritzi, we sit over there." She points to a table in the far corner of the cafeteria. An undesirable location.

This is crazy. It would be easy to go with Bethany and plead ignorance of the pecking order at my new school. It would all be forgotten, and I could move on with my life. A life where no one respects me. My grandmother used to tell me that a princess doesn't get respect only because of who she is, but because of how she behaves. If you want respect, you need to act like you deserve it.

"I like it here." I take another super casual sip of my water. "Why don't you and Kim and Miles come here?"

I'm not at all surprised when Bethany takes a step back, her eyes wide with fear, and declines. But seriously, is Miss Pink Hair such a big deal in this school that the other kids fear her? I know about popular. Even after only a month, I have lots of friends at Academie Sainte Marie, and not just because I'm a princess. You don't become popular by being feared. You just become feared.

"You have to leave now, Frizzy," Jasmine repeats.

I'm getting a bit tired of her new and improved nickname for me. Maybe I should leave. Even if I win, and Jasmine sits with me, it would be a very uncomfortable lunch hour. But I can't leave. If, on my first day at this school, I let Jasmine win, then I'll never have another chance to get back what I've lost. She'll have proven herself superior to me.

And she's not.

I don't move.

She dumps the contents of her tray on my head.

Pasta and cheese runs down my hair and onto my shirt. Around me, the lunchroom is completely silent, and I know everyone is staring. Staring at me, the new girl, who has a tray full of food on her head. I clench my jaw to keep from screaming and blink hard to keep a tear from escaping.

"What's going on here?" A teacher, an older man with sweat stains under his armpits, looks from me to Jasmine and back again.

"The new girl is sitting in my seat," Jasmine says.

"I think you and I should take a trip to the office to see Mr. Lee," he says to Jasmine and then glances my way again. "Perhaps someone can show you the way to the nurse's office so you can get cleaned up."

There is no way I'm going to be able to get cleaned up in the nurse's office, and everyone knows it. Bethany takes the hint though. “Come on, Fritzi, I’ll show you where the nurse is.”

So, finally I’m out of the seat, and the chair doesn’t even have a chance to get cold before Jasmine’s friends are sitting at the table.

People stare at me as I walk out of the room, and some of them laugh. This would never happen to Georgie. But how could I have prevented it? If I’d given in and left the table, Jasmine would have won. And in the end, she won anyway. Is there any way to win against someone willing to dump her lunch on me and get sent to the principal’s office?

“I told you she was a jerk,” Bethany says.

“I will not stand for this.”

Bethany shakes her head. “It’s not even worth trying. She’s untouchable.”

“No one is untouchable.” If I, princess of Colsteinburg, can get a plate of macaroni dumped on me, then no one is untouchable.

Bethany doesn’t answer. Clearly, she doesn’t believe me. She opens a door marked “Nurse” and says, “I have to go finish my lunch. I guess I’ll see you later.” And she’s off.

Even the nice girl doesn’t want to be associated with me now that Jasmine has made me a target. Great. We better go home soon before I start an international incident by having every twelve-year-old in this state hate me.

The nurse, who looks like she’s barely out of college, sits at her desk eating yogurt. “Oh my, what happened to you?”

“Jasmine.”

She nods as if that is all the information she needs. "Do you want to try to get cleaned up, or should we call your mom and you can go home?"

I should be able to tough this out. As Shakespeare says in *A Midsummer's Night Dream*, "Though she be but little, she is fierce."

Pap used to quote that to me.

Don't think of him in the past tense. Pap will quote that to me again. And soon.

But I am feisty; I am fierce; I am Fritzi. I can do this.

It's just hard with cheese in my hair.

"I want to go home," I say.

Henri picks me up and doesn't ask for explanations, which is good. I don't have to explain anything to him. Georgie, on the other hand, wants to know what happened. As soon as we get home, she hurries me into our room and shuts the door.

"What happened?" she asks, sounding more annoyed than sympathetic.

I tell her all about Jasmine and her meanness and her calling me Frizzy and not letting me sit where I wanted to sit. "It's not at all what I expected," I say, trying not to let any tears escape.

"What did you expect?" Georgie asks, a touch more sympathy in her voice. "To be treated like a princess?"

"Of course." I'm surprised she even has to ask that. "I am a princess."

"They don't know that," Georgie points out.

Only because we haven't told them, but shouldn't it be obvious without us having to say anything?

"Grandpa used to say that being a princess was about more than a title. It's how we act and who we are inside. He said we glow from within."

"He didn't really mean you glowed," Georgie says.

"I know that. But ..."

"Listen, Fritzi, and listen good," Georgie says. She takes hold of my shoulders and makes me look at her. "Princess is just a title. Like king. It doesn't confer special powers. It doesn't make you different than anyone else, especially here in America."

"But ..."

"No."

Georgie never gets this firm with me. Maybe it's best to leave it for now, but what I want to know is if king and queen and princess are just titles, then how come Mam got lost inside herself when her title was jeopardized?

"Go take a shower," Georgie says softly. "I'll tell Mam you had a shortened day today."

I wish we didn't have to hide the details from Mam. I want to tell her everything that happened today and have her comfort me and tell me it will be all right.

As I dry off, a sudden pang of longing for Mademoiselle

Colette comes over me. She might not have been the most imaginative nanny, no matter how many times I tried to get her to watch *Mary Poppins* to give her more ideas, but she was always sympathetic. What would she tell me to do if I went to her with this problem? She'd probably tell me to hold my head high and remember who I am.

That's the thing, all my life I've been told to live up to who I am. I couldn't do some things and had to do others because I was Princess Fredericka. Now I can't even tell people who I am. I suppose just because other people don't know, it doesn't mean I'm not still a princess. So, the answer: Hold my head high and behave like the princess I know I am.

CHAPTER 10

Today is going to be a better day than yesterday. I am a princess, even if I am currently a princess in exile, and I resolve to remember to act like one. With my hair pulled back in a braid, wearing my favorite pair of jeans and a Snoopy T-shirt, I head out to school with Henri as my escort.

In Spanish class, Señora Sanchez not-so-nicely reminds me that I have not covered my book yet.

In math, I get a lecture on the importance of doing homework, something I gave no thought to last night.

In gym, I change into the shorts and T-shirt that Henri bought me on a school supply shopping expedition yesterday and join the rest of the class for basketball. I am not surprised to be placed on the team with Bethany. I'm sure the teacher figures that team can't get any worse, so why not put the new kid there?

When I take up my position on the court, Jasmine is opposite me.

"I'm taking you out, Frizzy," she says. "You're going down."

I smile. She doesn't scare me. Much.

"I don't think so, Pinkie."

The gym teacher blows a whistle, and our game starts. I've never played basketball before, but I did spend yesterday watching, and I think I've got the basics down. Someone passes the ball to me, and I immediately look for someone else to pass it to, like I would do in netball. No one is available, and I remember that I can move with the ball as long as I dribble. I start to bounce the ball, and Jasmine steals it from me.

That will not happen again.

And it doesn't.

I intercept the ball when she's passing it to someone else on her team and take a shot at the basket. The ball goes in, and I grin. I can do this.

There's one girl on my team who knows what she's doing, and she seems relieved to have someone else putting in an effort. We pass the ball back and forth between us, taking turns at the basket. We let Bethany and her friends fade into the background, as they'd apparently like to do.

We don't win. Jasmine's team outperforms us, but that's okay. I didn't make a fool of myself, and Jasmine didn't make a fool of me. In fact, I showed Jasmine that I wasn't someone to be messed with. As far as that goes, I feel the game was a success.

"I didn't know you could play basketball," Bethany says as we head to lunch.

"I didn't know either," I say. "I never played it before today."

"But you're so good," she says. I'm not sure if she's impressed or annoyed.

"I play netball. It's similar," I say.

"Is that what they played in your old school? In France?" she asks.

"*Oui*," I say, because apparently I can't help myself speaking French when I think of Academie Sainte Marie. "I mean yes."

"I know what *oui* means," she says. "I'm not stupid."

Okay, then.

Bethany goes off to buy her lunch, and I head straight for the sunny table again. Jasmine didn't take me down in gym, and she won't take me down here.

This time, no one warns me or even really looks at me. Everyone seems to be very carefully looking at other things. Maybe it's because they don't want to see me get food dumped on my head again.

My stomach is in knots, but I take a bite of my bologna sandwich and wash it down with a swallow of water as I wait for Jasmine to make her next move. Hopefully, whatever they serve for lunch today isn't too messy. Maybe it will be a nice turkey sandwich or something that I can simply brush off.

The conversation around me fades to a buzz, and I know

Jasmine is approaching. I count to ten before looking up—no reason to make her think I'm waiting for her. She's got a death glare focused on me, and I cringe when I see chili on her plate. This could get ugly.

I smile my most plastic princess smile, the one I use when meeting dignitaries who bore me to pieces. "Hello, Jasmine, please have a seat. It's a shame you didn't get to eat your lunch yesterday. We wouldn't want that to happen again." I take another bite of my sandwich, hoping it isn't too obvious that my hands are shaking.

Venom leaks from her voice when she answers me. "Why are you at this table again?"

I take a deep breath and summon my inner princess. A feeling of calm comes over me. I've got this.

"I like this table."

"Are you crazy?" one of the girls surrounding Jasmine asks. She reminds me of Claudia with her curly blond hair and tiny nose.

I simply smile and take another sip of my water. Maybe I am crazy. But I refuse to curl up and be walked all over by anyone.

"This is our table," Jasmine says, implying perhaps that I haven't already gotten that impression.

I wave toward all the empty seats. "Sit down. Please."

Jasmine puts the tray down, and the tightness in my chest relaxes a little. Maybe I won't have chili dumped on me after all.

"Listen, Frizzy," she says, hands on hips. "This is our table, and we don't want you sitting here. So move."

I take another swallow of water to steady myself. "The name is Fritzi. And if you don't want to sit with me, sit somewhere else. I'm sitting here. You might as well join me."

The girl who looks like Claudia sits down. "This is silly," she says to Jasmine. "Just sit. We can ignore her."

"That's not the point," Jasmine says, but she sits. They all do and eat their lunch without another word to me.

I guess I won, but somehow I thought victory would taste sweeter.

As soon as the bell rings, Jasmine and her friends dash from the table, in an attempt, I guess, to get as far away from me as possible. I throw out my lunch bag and look at my schedule.

Bethany comes over to me, arms crossed. "Do you want me to show you where geography is, or would you rather follow your new friends?" There's a coldness in her voice that wasn't there before.

"I'd like you to show me," I say. "I can hardly call those girls my friends."

"Then why sit at their table?"

"Because I like that table."

"There are plenty of fine tables where you can sit without having Jasmine bother you. Why don't you sit with us? I thought we were getting along."

"You've been wonderful!" I assure her, because I can't afford to lose the one person who's been friendly to me in this school. "But I can't let her win."

Bethany gives a sad shake of her head. "Jasmine always wins. The sooner you accept that, the happier you'll be."

"Wrong on both counts. I don't intend to lose. And if I did, I'd never be happy."

"Must be hard being you," Bethany says.

"You have no idea," I say, which I don't think is the response she expected. I follow her to geography and am less than thrilled to see Jasmine and friends lounging in the back row seats.

"Oh look, Frizzy is in this class too," Jasmine says. "Wonderful."

One of the main problems with red hair is that it tends to go along with fair skin, the kind of skin that changes to red very quickly. Right now, I know my cheeks are flaming.

"It's Fritzi," I say through clenched teeth. "Can't you get that through your little pink head, or do you perhaps have a speech impediment that prevents you from saying my name properly?"

Jasmine quirks an eyebrow at that. "If anyone can't talk, it's you. What kind of an accent is that, anyway?"

"Cultured," I say and sit down in the closest available seat.

Bethany has ducked her head and refuses to look in my direction. That's fine, I don't need her to fight my battles for me. Though if she really wants to be my friend, it would be nice if she had my back on this.

The teacher walks in and starts class. The lecture is on the location of the countries in Europe. I've got this. I take half-hearted notes and wonder when Sophia is going to return my text.

The end-of-class bell almost drowns out the ringing of my phone, but the teacher still hears it.

"You can't have that phone on during school hours, Miss Moore," he says.

"No problem," I say. "I'll turn it off." One glance at the phone tells me this is Sophia. I can't miss this call. I slip into the hall with the rest of the class and answer it. It's too loud in the hall to hear anything, so I duck into the girls' restroom.

"Sophia?" I press the phone to my ear.

"I shouldn't be talking to you," she says in French, because it's the language we use at school.

"You have to help me," I answer, also in French.

"Fritzi, I can't," she says, and she sounds the tiniest bit regretful.

The bathroom door opens, and Jasmine strides in and stares at me. I turn my back; I don't need to deal with her right now.

"We can get them to see reason."

"I think my father is perfectly reasonable. The monarchy has run its course."

"But ..."

"My father has forbidden me to speak to you, but you were my friend, and I didn't want to not say *adieu*."

Were? My throat suddenly feels swollen.

"*Adieu*?" I ask. It comes out as almost a whisper.

"*Oui. Adieu. Bon courage*." Sophia says quietly, and then the line goes dead.

I pocket the phone, wipe the wetness from my eyes, and turn

to see Jasmine still staring at me.

"Quel est le problème?"

She looks at me blankly, and I realize I'm still speaking French. "What's your problem?" I repeat, in English this time.

"You," she says and pushes past me.

"Oh, that's original."

She inspects her flawless reflection in the mirror, while applying lip gloss. "Was that French?"

"Oui."

"If you speak French, why are you taking Spanish?"

Exactly what I want to know. "The school seems to think since I can already speak French, I need to learn Spanish."

"Typical." Jasmine puts her lip gloss away and then frowns at me, as if realizing she has been civil to me. She pushes past me to the door. "You're going to make me late for class," she says and leaves.

My world may be falling down around me, but there's no reason to make it worse by my being late to class either. I leave the bathroom to find Bethany waiting for me like a faithful servant.

"Everything okay?" she asks.

Not even a little bit, but it isn't like I can discuss it with her. "Fine," I say. "Where do we go next?"

I follow Bethany to English, where once again, Jasmine is enthroned at the back of the class. I brace myself to hear her call me Frizzy again, but she says nothing.

I slip into an empty seat and wait for class to begin, but my mind isn't on English class. All I can think about is Sophia's quiet *adieu*. What does that mean? She's simply cutting me off, siding with her father? Does this mean I have to be enemies with my best friend? I can't do that.

I wish I knew what was going on at home. Has anything changed since Georgie and I checked last night? How can I find out?

"We'll be going to the media center," Mrs. Howe announces, "so you can get started on your research projects."

Score! A perfect chance to do a little research on my own.

"Fritzi, you'll have to choose a topic. It can be anything at all, as long as you have at least three sources and can write five pages on it."

I follow the rest of the class through the halls to the media center, or as they call it at Sainte Marie, *la bibliothèque*. We are each handed a laptop out of a cabinet and told to find a place to set up. I choose a table in the corner, away from everyone else, and wait for the machine to boot up.

The first thing I do is search online for Colsteinburg, like I do every time I get the chance.

There are pictures of protesters and riots and general chaos. I want to cry as I see my beloved home looking so hurt. But are these people protesting Pap or Orcutt's attempted takeover? Where is Pap? Why are there no articles about the speeches he's giving trying to bring calm? Isn't he giving those speeches? Shouldn't he be?

There is a headline, "Where is the royal family?"

I click on it, and a picture of me and Georgie with our parents pops up. It's from the night of the ball, and looking at it makes me want to cry. We look like the perfect, happy royal family. What happened?

"That's you!"

I slam the laptop shut, making all eyes turn toward me.

CHAPTER 11

Bethany sits beside me. "Wasn't that you in the picture?" she asks.

From across the room the teacher calls to me, "Is there a problem?"

"*Non*." I close my eyes so I can concentrate on my words and switch to English. "Not at all," I say. "Sorry, I got startled."

"We need to treat these machines with care. They are expensive."

"Right. Sorry," I repeat.

Bethany is still sitting next to me.

"Well?" she asks, arms crossed.

"I don't know what you're talking about," I lie.

"That picture you were looking at. It was you."

"Can't you just let me do my work?" Maybe it's not the most diplomatic response, but I don't have good answers for her, and I want to look at the article without her interference.

"Fine," Bethany says, sounding as if it is anything but fine. I don't mean to hurt her feelings, but some things are more important right now—like what that article says.

She moves on, and I reopen the computer. The article tells how the royal family has not been seen since the night of the coup. Cold shivers go up my arms. Where is Pap? We left him there to settle things. Why has no one seen him? What happened to him?

There is speculation about what happened to the royal family. No one seems to suspect that the queen and princesses have left the country and are alive and well in America. Multiple rumors have us dead or imprisoned. The really disturbing thing is that the people who think we're dead don't seem horribly upset by the idea. It's like we're characters on a TV show or something. But we're real, and if we were dead, I'd like to think it would matter to someone.

I want to show the people of Colsteinburg that we are not dead. It's almost as bad that we're in hiding. It's our country. Why didn't we stay and fight for it?

I click to another part of the article. There are pictures of mobs and riots in the streets. A car burns in front of Berg's Apothetik. It's so unreal.

I don't hear the teacher come up behind me.

"What topic have you chosen for your research paper, Fritzi?"

Mrs. Howe asks, and I jump.

"Military coups and revolutions," I answer without thinking.

"That's rather broad. You might want to narrow it down a bit." She leans closer to the screen. Her glasses, dangling from a chain around her neck, hit me in the back of the head. I move the pointer so I can close the browser window, but she might take that as a sign that I am looking at something inappropriate. I leave it as it is.

"What's that all about?" she asks. "Some kind of protest?"

"*Ja,* something like that," I say, and she moves on to the next student.

Does she seriously not know what these pictures are of? It is clearly a crowd in front of our palace. It isn't like it's some generic side street that could be anywhere in the world. Doesn't she know that the whole social fabric of Colsteinburg is being ripped apart? Doesn't she care?

I know our country is small, but doesn't a coup warrant worldwide news?

I take out a notebook. I'm going to research the coup in Colsteinburg for my paper. Maybe that way I'll be able to figure out how to fix everything.

There isn't much more information than Georgie and I found the other day. Francisco Orcutt wants a modern government and thinks the monarchy is a relic of the middle ages. He thinks it's time for an elected head of state, and he, naturally, wants to be that head.

A group of royalists led by Ivan Frank, who drove us to the airport in the beat-up Honda, are making the case for keeping things the way they've been.

Heated debate fills the comboxes and, judging by the pictures, has spilled over into the streets.

I see no official word from Pap. Shouldn't he be out there showing why we still need a monarchy? What if something has happened to him? What if that's the reason he's not saying anything? I take out my phone and send him a text.

Are you okay? I love you.

I don't know if he'll get it, but if he does, at least he'll know we're thinking about him.

Since there don't seem to be too many details on what's going on in Colsteinburg, I look up other coups and insurrections, to try to get a sense of how things played out. Things seldom end peacefully, which is something I'd prefer not to think about.

The bell rings. I have two more classes, science and cooking. I look for Bethany to show me the way, since she did say we had all our classes together, but she's already walking out of the library. I gather my books and ask Mrs. Howe how to get to the science classroom.

Jasmine is not enthroned in the back row of this class. She's not here at all. That will make it less stressful, I'm sure, but also probably a little boring.

There's a seat open next to Bethany, and I head to it.

"Is it okay if I sit here?" I ask.

"Suit yourself," Bethany says.

Great. I've totally alienated her just because I didn't want to talk about those pictures. She's the only one who's been nice to me here, and I want to make it up to her somehow. I sit down and lean close to her.

"That was a picture of me," I say, "but please don't tell anyone."

"Why?" she asks. "What's the big secret?"

Do people here really not have any idea what is going on back home?

"It's just ... I really can't explain," I finish lamely. Maybe she didn't realize it was a picture of the royal family, in which case she won't be likely to give me away, but how can I explain why things need to be kept quiet without revealing myself? This is all too hard. I just want to be myself.

"When was the picture taken?" she asks.

"Last Saturday," I say. Doesn't seem to be any harm in admitting that.

"Where are you from, really?" she asks.

That I can't answer.

Luckily, the teacher starts class, and I have a perfectly good excuse for not saying anything.

Bethany seems to have forgiven me because she shows me to the last class of the day: cooking, where we learn to boil water and cook pasta. Skills I don't have and which, unfortunately, might prove useful one of these days.

All in all, it's a pretty good school day, and after I stash the books I don't need in my locker, securing it with my new lock, I go outside and see Georgie there waiting to walk me home.

"How'd it go today?" she asks.

"Not bad," I say. "Where's Henri?"

"Home with Mam. I convinced him it was safe enough for me to come for you on my own. I needed to get out."

Poor Georgie. Life has to be really boring for her here. She graduated from Academie Sainte Marie in the spring. Her days lately have been busy with social engagements, since she was already beginning to fulfill her duties as next in line for the throne. Doing nothing must be driving her crazy.

"Have you heard anything from Pap?"

"He called Mam," Georgie says.

He called! That means he is alive and well. He'll get my text message and know we miss him. But he called, and I wasn't there to talk to him.

"I missed it! If you didn't make me go to school, I would have been there." I stamp my foot. It isn't fair.

Georgie puts a hand on my arm. "I didn't talk to him either. He only talked to Mam for a couple of minutes. It was all he could manage."

Oh. I still wish I'd been there.

"What did he say?"

"All I know," Georgie says, "is that things are difficult right now."

"Is he going to send the military after them?"

"After who?"

"The protesters. Isn't that what they did in Egypt and some other places?" My research this afternoon taught me a thing or two.

"And if you recall, that didn't work out so well in those places. In most of those cases, the person in office was overthrown."

"Oh." True, that was what my research showed me. "Then how do we stop them? How does Pap take control again? Can't he put them in jail or something?"

"I don't know," Georgie admits. "I don't think it's as simple as that."

"What if we went back there, you and me, and talked to the people? Maybe we could get them to see reason. They like us. Especially you. People would listen to you."

Georgie's lips turn up in a sad half smile. "I don't know. Maybe they don't like us as much as we thought." She pulls out her phone and shows me an article that has a picture of the two of us in our finery at the ball and a picture of some children living in squalor. The caption is "Royal family squandered money while children suffered."

"But," I sputter. "That's not fair. We don't have such poverty in Colsteinburg."

"Shh," Georgie warns.

We stop at the corner, and a crowd gathers around, all waiting for the light to change. Once we are safely across the street, and a reasonable distance from anyone else, Georgie continues.

"It's not about what's fair. The point is, we may not be as

popular as we thought we were. I'm not sure going back there would be smart. Or safe," she adds as an afterthought.

But I can picture it. I'd wear my school uniform so I look appropriately young and innocent. I'd stand out on the balcony that Pap uses to make his public appearances. I'd tell the crowd that they are wrong, that Pap is a good king. I'd make them understand that he is doing all he can for people. It isn't like he can solve all the problems in the world. Mr. Orcutt isn't going to be able to solve all the problems either. No one can. So why change when things are really working rather well? We are a peaceful country, left to ourselves, uninvolved in wars. Maybe the economy isn't as strong as it could be, but if we all work together we can solve that.

It might work.

"Listen," Georgie says as we walk up the three steps to the front door of our borrowed home. "Mam doesn't like to talk about any of this. Better just not to bring it up, okay?"

I nod. I'm not happy about it, and I don't understand why Mam is acting this way, but I can do my part not to make things worse.

Mam is sitting on the sofa in jeans and a T-shirt, watching TV, when we go in. "Hi, Mam," I say. She looks up briefly, as if to see who spoke to her, and switches her attention back to the TV. This is not the Mam I know and love. It scares me.

Henri is in the kitchen, an apron wrapped around his waist, cutting up vegetables. I almost laugh, but he is holding a knife, so

I manage to control myself.

"Are you a chef, Henri?" I ask.

"I have many hidden talents, Your Royal Highness," he answers.

Georgie opens the refrigerator and grabs two sodas, handing one to me. We sit at the little kitchen table.

"We need to get Mam home," I say, popping open the soda. "She's like a mermaid without water. A queen without her kingdom. She can't survive."

"Her Majesty must stay here, where it's safe," Henri says.

"You could keep us safe back home, Henri. We trust you," I say.

Henri gives a nod in acknowledgment and says, "I appreciate your trust in me, but the situation is such that I don't know that to be true."

"Henri is right," Georgie says. "You heard the crowd that night."

"Then why can't we tell anyone where we are? The mob is in Colsteinburg, not here."

Georgie sighs, and I can tell she's trying to decide if she should tell me something or not. She looks at Henri, who answers for her.

"His Majesty wants to make sure that no one can use you in their attempt to take over the country."

"Use us?" I ask. "Like make us do a TV commercial for the other side or something?"

"Threaten to hurt us so Pap does what they want," Georgie explains bluntly. "Kidnap us."

Oh.

Maybe it is better to stay here and safe.

"So just let Pap do what he needs to do. He needs to know we're all safe here. Okay?"

I nod, a lump in my throat. I don't want Pap to have to worry about us as well as everything else.

CHAPTER 12

The weekend passes uneventfully, which I guess is good. At least I have some homework to keep me occupied. I never thought I'd think homework was a good thing—this is the level we've been brought down to.

Monday morning, Georgie puts a bologna sandwich and a bottle of water in a brown paper bag for me.

"Can't I have a different kind of sandwich?" I ask.

Georgie leans against the counter, arms crossed. She looks tired. "It's what we've got. I'll see if Henri can take me to the store later and get something else. But for right now, just deal with it, okay?"

"I wish we were home," I say.

"I do too," Georgie admits.

The defeated way she says it doesn't make me feel much better.

I finish my cereal and put the bowl in the dishwasher. Henri is in the doorway, ready to escort me to school.

School. The last place I feel like being today.

"You better get going," Georgie says. "I'll see you later."

I'm so preoccupied with thinking of ways I can help Pap save the kingdom that in Spanish class, I answer all the questions in French, which amuses Jasmine to no end but annoys Señora Sanchez.

At lunchtime, I'm not in the mood for a battle of wills with Jasmine, so I sit with Bethany and her friends.

"So, the princess has decided to grace us with her presence?" Miles asks, a touch of a sneer in his voice.

"What?" I nearly drop my lunch. How did they find out? Did Bethany go looking for that picture and figure out who we really are?

"He just means since you've been sitting with Jasmine and company, he figured you were too good to sit with us," Bethany clarifies.

"Oh." I sit down, willing my heartbeat to return to normal.

"Why aren't you sitting with the A Team today?" Kim asks. "Didn't they want you?"

What have I done to earn this animosity from people I thought liked me?

"I thought it would be nice to sit with people who might actually talk to me. But I can go someplace else if that's a problem."

"You won't let Jasmine scare you off, but you'll let Kim chase you away? No one is afraid of Kim," Miles says, opening a bag of chips.

"It's true," Kim says. "No one is afraid of me. People usually don't even apologize if they bump into me. I think sometimes they don't even see me."

I have never felt invisible. People always knew who I was and where I was and were quick to pay attention to me when I entered the room. After all, I am Princess Fredericka, and something like that gets you noticed. But now, people don't know me, don't care who I am or what I am doing. I have more in common with Kim than I would have thought possible.

I pull out my bologna sandwich and sigh. I want the lunches that our cook prepared, with hot soup and fresh bread. Even the lunches in the dining hall at Sainte Marie's were much more exciting than my bologna on white bread. If we have to stay in exile for long, I might starve.

"You finally saw the error of your ways?" Jasmine stands over me, an evil little smile on her face. "Went to the loser table, where you belong?"

"No, I simply decided I didn't want to sit with you anymore. You bore me." I go back to my even more boring sandwich, pretending I am super interested in it.

Out of the corner of my eye, I can see Jasmine turning red and spluttering. "I bore you!" She can barely get the words out. "You're like the queen of boring."

My back stiffens at that, but I say nothing.

"And you don't even have a good lunch. How disgusting. What is that? Some weird meat on white bread?"

I frown. While I totally agree with her, I can't let her know that.

"Surely you've heard of bologna, haven't you? It's a royal meat first instituted by the Duke of Bologna in the Middle Ages. It's been a staple of the Italian royal family ever since then." I am totally making all that up.

"Well," she says, suddenly a little unsure of herself. "It still looks disgusting."

"*Ja*, a little," I admit. "But a girl's got to eat."

Jasmine doesn't respond to that but heads to her favored table. Tomorrow, I'll probably sit there again, just to mess with her.

Kim, Miles, and Bethany are all staring at me.

"What?" Do I have ketchup on my chin or something?

"How did you do that?" Kim asks, her eyes wide.

"What?"

"Leave Jasmine speechless. No one does that." Awe is apparent in her voice.

"And that bit about bologna, that was pure baloney," Miles says.

"*Ja*, I know."

"It's not from Italy," Miles continues. "It's as American as you or I."

"Actually, it is from Italy," I say, "and I'm—" I stop myself. It's better if they think I'm American. That is one way of hiding our true identities, right? "Anyway, I bet she'll want bologna now, so she can be like Italian royalty."

"Well, like I told you, she already thinks she's a princess," Bethany says.

Jasmine and I have that much in common anyway. I concentrate on my sandwich, and soon lunch is over.

In English class, we go back to the media center again to work on our projects. Bethany sits next to me, and I try not to show that I'd rather be alone. Alienating my only friend is not a good plan.

My heart aches as I look up information about my country. Every picture I see, every comment I read, reminds me that I am a world away and helpless to do anything.

I should have chosen another topic for my research paper. Something that wouldn't make my stomach hurt when I researched it. Something like Koalas Are the Cutest Animals or Why Does Soda Taste So Good.

Across the room, Jasmine and her friends break into giggles. I look, sure they are laughing at me. It seems to be the way Jasmine operates. But I can see Jasmine's computer screen, and it appears they are watching videos. They aren't laughing at me after all.

"They're going to get in trouble," Bethany whispers to me. "They are supposed to be doing research, not watching videos."

I don't really care if they get in trouble. In fact, I would rather enjoy it, but a thought is beginning to form in my head. I need to get the word out that the royal family is alive and well and that we intend to stay the royal family. I can't go back to Colsteinburg to tell people in person. I was able to be convincing about bologna, and that wasn't even true. How much more convincing could I be for something that I really care about?

Everyone is afraid that the opposition will try to use us to help them. Why not beat them to it? I will make a video convincing the people of Colsteinburg not to follow Orcutt.

The solution is so simple; why didn't I think of it before?

I can't wait for the school day to end so I can go back to the condo and put my plan into action. Finally, there is something I can do to help Pap.

When the last bell finally rings and I go outside, it's not Georgie waiting for me, but Henri.

"Is that your father?" Bethany asks. I didn't even realize she was at my elbow until she spoke.

"No," I say.

"Stepfather?" she persists.

"Um, no." There is really no good way to explain who Henri is without giving away who we are. I wish Bethany wouldn't ask so many questions.

"But he is here to pick you up, right? I mean, he's waving to you."

"Yes, he's here for me," I say.

"It's not like you're meeting some stranger off the internet or anything, are you?" Bethany asks. "That can be really dangerous."

"He's not a stranger." I sigh. How easy it would be just to say he's in charge of my mother, the queen's, security. But I'm not supposed to tell anyone who we are. "It's fine. I have to go."

"I hope you don't mind walking," Henri says. "It's a beautiful day. I thought the exercise would be good."

"Yeah, whatever." I don't care if we walk or drive a car or ride camels. I only want to know one thing. "Where's Georgie?"

"She did not feel up to going out in public this afternoon."

That's not like Georgie. "What happened?" Did the stress finally get to her? Is she going to get lost inside herself like Mam? What will I do?

"Something to do with Prince Etienne, I believe," Henri says, his voice low so as to not be overheard.

"You have to tell me," I insist. He does, once we are closer to the townhouse and away from curious ears.

"Princess Georgiana saw a picture of Etienne with a French model. The caption said that he had moved on."

Poor Georgie! I practically run the rest of the way home so I can get to her and comfort her.

I find her in our bedroom, lying on her back, staring at the ceiling.

"Henri told me," I say. "I'm sure it's just a big misunderstanding." I sit on the edge of the bed. "Have you contacted him?"

"How can I contact him when we're not supposed to let anyone know where we are?"

"You don't have to tell him where we are," I say. "I didn't tell

Sophia when I texted her."

Georgie sits up so suddenly I jump. "You texted Sophia?" The horror in her voice makes me think that maybe that wasn't a good plan.

"Yes?" I try to make myself small. It seemed like such a good idea at the time.

"Why?" Georgie demands.

"I thought we could work together to convince her father he's wrong, and then everything could get back to normal."

"How could you be so foolish?"

That's not fair. I stand up.

"Now, wait a minute. I was trying to help. No one else seems to be doing anything. Besides, we're not supposed to be talking about me but about how you can fix things with Etienne."

Georgie doesn't say anything right away, so I continue. "Besides, nothing horrible happened when I texted Sophia. I'm sure it's fine to send Etienne a message."

She shakes her head and lies back down on the bed. "Just let me be, please."

It seems like the best course of action.

I go down to the kitchen and get myself a soda. Mam is sitting on the sofa, a cup of coffee in front of her. The TV is off.

"Nothing good on TV?" I ask.

"It's all the same. It gets tedious after a while."

It's refreshing that she's realized it. Maybe that means she'll start being Mam again.

"You're used to being busy," I say. "You need to find something to keep you busy."

"There is nothing," Mam says. "We can only sit here, aimlessly, waiting."

I can't. I can't just sit here. "I'm going outside," I say.

"Take Henri with you," Mam says.

"I'm just going outside," I say. "I don't need a bodyguard."

I take my soda out to the front steps, where I try to figure out the next part of my plan.

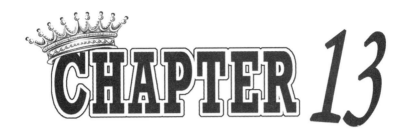

CHAPTER 13

I need to make that video. One thing I learned from my research is that the way a coup is stopped is if the military is on the side of the king. I'm not sure how the military feels about the king right now, but the military is made up of people, of citizens. So, I need to convince the citizens to stick by the royal family.

How do I do that?

I take another sip of my soda and then look at the can with its readily recognizable design. I've been all over the world and am always able to find this brand of soda. How did they make people all over the world like them? What is their secret?

I take out my phone and watch a few of their commercials from around the world. They are all short, upbeat, and happy, and they make you sure that the one thing that will make a good life even better is if you share their soda with someone.

Maybe I can make that work for me.

I would prefer to make this video in the privacy of my bedroom, but Georgie is up there, pouting. Mam and Henri are in the living room. There aren't too many places to go in this townhouse for privacy. But no one is out and about on the street. Maybe the front step is private enough.

Short. Sweet. Upbeat. I can do that.

I put my camera on video and hold it out in front of me. Holding my can of soda in the other hand, I smile and start speaking in German.

"*Hallo!* Prinzessin Fredericka here. Some say the royal family has abandoned Colsteinburg. That is not true." Okay, maybe in the most literal sense, since most of us aren't on her soil, it is true, but we didn't abandon her in our hearts, and that's what counts. "We are alive and well and as devoted to Colsteinburg and her people as always." What else to say? I have to be quick about this. "Until we are together again, *Prost!*" I say, giving the German equivalent of "cheers," and I take a sip.

And cut. End of video. I watch it and decide it's not too bad. I upload it to my social media accounts. Now I just have to wait and see if it makes a difference.

At least I'm doing something to help.

Hopefully it works.

The door opens, and Henri stands there. For a second I think he's already seen the video and is going to chastise me, but he seems surprised to find me sitting on the step.

"Everything all right, Your Royal Highness?" he asks.

"It's fine, Henri. Thanks," I say. Better than all right.

"Your mother was wondering if you have homework you should be doing."

"Probably," I answer.

"I was wondering if you would like to go out for ice cream."

I grin. "Yes!" I jump up.

At least Henri understands that I need to get out of that condo now and then.

I almost tell Henri about the video as we sit and eat our sundaes, but something holds me back. He'll probably tell me I should just wait things out and not get involved. Well, I'm tired of waiting, and it's too late for that now.

"You aren't worried about our safety?" I say, as I look around at the handful of people in the ice cream place.

"I am always worried about your safety," he answers. "It's my job. But I think no one knows you are here. It is safe."

"It's only safe if no one knows we are here?" I ask. "But I'm going to school. People know I'm there."

"But people don't know who you really are," Henri says softly. "Right?"

I nod, swallowing hard. "Right."

"And it's going to stay that way, right?"

As long as no one from school sees the videos. But why would any of them look at the Princess Fredericka account? I'm good,

I'm sure I am.

We go back to the townhouse, and Henri cooks dinner. Georgie even comes down, although she looks a lot paler than I like to see her. This exile is not good for her at all. Hopefully my video will have an impact quickly.

I'm not expecting that impact to be at school.

Jasmine stops by my desk in homeroom and puts her phone on top of my books. I see my video playing on her screen.

"Prinzessin Fredericka?"

Oh.

"*Ja*," I say. There's no point in lying. It's right there on her phone.

"What's that even mean?"

"Take your seat, Jasmine, so I can take attendance," the teacher says.

I almost want to stand up in the front of the class and tell them that I'm a princess, for real, and be able to be myself again, but I don't get that chance. As the morning continues, I notice looks and whispers, but most people keep their opinions to themselves. I wish they wouldn't. I want to know what they are saying about me.

"I thought you were just a normal kid," Bethany says to me in Spanish class.

"I'm not," I say, and I'm not ashamed of it.

Bethany turns back to her books without saying anything else. Perhaps she's one of those people who gets shy around royalty. I've met people like that before. Usually, once I have a chance to talk to them and they get to know me, they relax again. But Bethany already knows me, and I don't get a chance to say anything else before class begins.

I don't know if Señora Sanchez has heard the rumors that I'm a princess, but she seems surprised when I answer questions correctly in her class. She shouldn't be. After all, I speak English, German, and French. Learning beginner Spanish isn't really that hard.

In math, I lose myself in equations, and suddenly I understand why Georgie finds peace in doing calculus: There is a problem; you can attack it logically, and there is an answer. It's nice to have answers.

In gym, Jasmine picks me for her basketball team. I feel a small surge of welcoming warmth when I go to stand behind her.

"I only chose you because you're good at this, not because you're a princess or I like you or anything," she mutters to me. The warmth cools a bit, but only a little.

"Naturally," I respond.

We win the game easily, and although I don't anticipate ever being best friends with Jasmine, since we won't be here long enough to develop real friendships, I do think she may refrain from dumping her food on me from now on.

At lunch, I head toward the table by the window. I sit and remove my sandwich—thankfully, not bologna—from my bag. When Jasmine and her friends arrive, they look resigned and sit without any complaint. Jasmine takes the seat right next to me.

"You're a princess?" one of her friends asks, and I realize I've sat with them several times already and don't know their names.

"I am," I say.

"Do you just mean that you're totally spoiled or something like that?" another asks.

"No," I say. "It means my father is king of Colsteinburg."

"Colsteinburg? Where's that?" the first girl asks.

"It's in the Alps," Jasmine says, her face a mask. "And it's been in the news a lot lately. The revolution. The missing royal family. The whole bit." I'm impressed she is so up on current events. "So, what are you doing here? Slumming?"

"Um, no," I say. "I'm here to go to school. My parents wanted my sister and me out of the country for our safety. As you said. Revolution and all that."

"Did you ever meet Prince Harry?" one of the other girls asks.

The question catches me a bit off guard; I was expecting something more about revolutions and social upheaval.

"Actually I have met him." I think of the picture that he signed "to my best girl," which I left in my room at home.

"So, are you rich? Do you live in a castle? Do you eat off of gold plates?"

"Usually we use regular china," I say. Though I have seen a set of gold plates, I don't think I should mention that. "We live in a palace. I guess you could say we're rich."

"Do you dress up in fancy clothes all the time?"

I remember my beautiful silk gown from the ball, and my

throat tightens a bit.

"Sometimes," I say. "When I'm at school, I wear a uniform."

"Ugh, uniforms!"

"It's not so bad."

"How come you dress like a slob now?" Jasmine asks.

"We left in a hurry," I say softly. I hate admitting to the fact that we ran away. "We didn't get time to think about what we were packing."

"That must have been scary," another girl says.

"*Ja*." I can feel tears building, and I don't want to cry in front of them. I'm a princess. I can do this.

"What's it like being a princess?" A thin girl with huge earrings asks.

What's it like? It's my life. "It's great," I say. "My family founded Colsteinburg eight hundred years ago, so my family history and the history of my country are completely intertwined. Everywhere Georgie—that's my sister—and I go, people want to see us and talk to us and take our picture. We get to go to all kinds of special events and private showings."

"There's no downside?" Jasmine asks.

There was one time a website announced Georgie was pregnant. That rumor spread like wildfire, and it took a bit of doing for King Franz to get everything settled down. There was the time last year when someone made a threat against me, and I had to be under constant guard for a week until they found out who it was and made sure everything was safe. Things weren't always perfect, but what is?

"I suppose," I say. "I mean, everything has its ups and downs, right?"

"When are you going home?" Jasmine asks. I try to read her body language and tone. Is she asking out of concern or because she wants me out of here? Maybe a little of both.

"As soon as we can manage it," I answer.

"Good," Jasmine says, but the bite is missing from her words. I glance at her, and she shrugs. "I mean, it's what you want, right?"

"Right."

This talk of my real life is making me homesick. I'm very happy when the bell rings and we get to go to the next class.

I sit in my usual seat next to Bethany. She glances at me and then looks away.

"I can explain," I say to her, though I'm not sure what I have to explain.

"Explain what? That you lied to all of us? Made fools of us?"

Maybe a case can be made for lies of omission, but how did I make fools of them?

"What are you talking about?" I ask.

"As if you didn't know," Bethany says. She stares straight ahead and doesn't look my way again before class starts.

Judging by the looks and whispers that follow me throughout the afternoon, everyone now knows I'm a princess. I expected things to get easier when people found out, but that doesn't seem to be the case. Most people don't talk to me about it, though; they simply stare and whisper.

I think I liked it better when I was just the new kid in school.

My head is pounding by the time the final bell rings. When I leave the school, there are news vans parked up and down the street and a phalanx of reporters with cameras, all apparently waiting for me.

This is not good. Not good at all.

I stand just outside the doors, trying to take it all in. Lots of kids mill around, maybe hoping to get on camera, maybe waiting to see what this is all about. They goof around and wave at cameras that are clearly off. One of the reporters spots me, and as if some sort of telepathic message goes between them all, the cameras point at me, red lights blinking. Before I can even process this, or wonder where Henri is, microphones are shoved in my face.

"Princess Fredericka, can you tell us what you are doing in Massachusetts?"

"Why did you leave Colsteinburg?"

"What is your opinion on what is happening in your country?"

Questions come at me fast and furious from all sides, and for the first time in my life, there is no one here to buffer me from them. I try to stand tall and proud like Georgie would, and I use a tried and true tactic I learned from my father for dealing with the press. Don't worry about answering the questions you are asked; answer the questions you wished they asked instead.

"Naturally, I'm eager to get back home, once all this unpleasantness has died down," I say.

"So, you think it will all simply blow over?"

Why anyone thinks asking a twelve-year-old political questions is a good idea, I can't imagine.

"Do you think it won't?" I ask, turning the question back around. I am media savvy enough to know not to answer something that could come back and bite me. Princesses don't just sit around learning how to embroider these days.

Then, out of nowhere, Henri is by my side. He gently takes my elbow. "Come, Your Royal Highness. The car is over here."

I've never been so happy to see someone.

We get in the car and lock the doors. I take a deep breath, but I know I'm still being watched and photographed, so I am careful about what my expression might give away.

"We need to talk," Henri says and holds up his phone so I can see my video playing.

CHAPTER 14

I wish my hands would stop shaking. Outside the window, the reporters and cameras are closing in on us. In the car, Henri is practically quivering with rage. There's no escape.

"Would you care to explain this, Your Royal Highness?"

"Shouldn't we get out of here?" I ask, hoping to put off the moment of reckoning a little longer.

"I'll drive. You talk." He pulls away from the school and artfully avoids the reporters and news vans and middle school kids standing with their mouths agape taking it all in. "Talk."

"I didn't want people to think we were dead or had abandoned them." That seems self-evident.

"Wasn't it made clear to you that you are in hiding? Does this look like hiding?"

"It's not like I told anyone where we are," I say.

"You didn't have to. Your phone did that for you."

Wait. What? Suddenly I feel a little light-headed.

"My phone did what?"

"It geo-tagged your video."

"Oh. I didn't know it could do that."

"It can do that."

I glance behind us at the trailing news vans. So, that's where they came from. They saw my video.

We get to the condo, and there are even more news vans there. Henri pulls up close to the door. "You don't have to talk to them," he says. "I will get you inside safely."

But wait, the news reporters have found us. There's not much point in pretending they haven't. And reporters can be our friends. I wanted to get the word out with my video that the royal family has not abandoned Colsteinburg and that there is a reason to fight for our familiar way of life. Well, a feature with a major news organization is even better than a fifteen-second video.

"I'm going to talk to them," I say.

"You are not," Henri responds, putting the car in park.

"I am." I hop out of the car, and immediately a woman with a microphone sticks it in front of my face. A man with a TV camera stands a little behind her, the red light on the camera plainly showing that he is recording. Georgie and I aren't exactly novices when it comes to dealing with the media. After all, we are the princesses of Colsteinburg. We are on TV at least once a month, though usually in a more controlled environment. I'm somewhat reassured that Henri is here.

"Princess Fredericka?"

"Yes," I say, hoping she can't see my shaking hands.

The door to the condo opens, and I half expect Henri to bodily pick me up and drag me inside. Instead, I find that Georgie is standing next to me.

"Princess Georgiana?" The woman asks, thrusting the microphone in Georgie's face.

Georgie puts on her practiced public smile. She is unflappable.

"Yes?" She answers, as sweetly as if an old woman had asked her to help pick up her dropped groceries or something.

"It really is you?" The woman seems surprised that she has it right.

"Of course," Georgie says, the smile not leaving her face. I notice it doesn't quite reach her eyes.

"Why aren't you in Colsteinburg?" the reporter asks.

Georgie and I exchange a quick look.

"Your Royal Highnesses, please come inside," Henri says, frustration evident in his voice.

Georgie nods, but then answers the question anyway. "Our father thought that, under the circumstances, we should be somewhere else for the time being. I'm sure you can agree that was a prudent move."

"And what is your opinion on what is happening in your home country?"

"I think you'd be better off asking policy questions from someone other than a couple of teenagers," Georgie answers, the smile never wavering.

"And where is your mother, Queen Cassandra?" the reporter asks.

For the first time, Georgie falters somewhat. Do we tell them Mam is here with us or not? Which looks better, that Mam stayed with us or with the country?

"She's inside," I say, making a split-second decision. "Of course. We're kids, our parents wouldn't send us out on our own. But she's got a sick headache today. Please just leave her be."

"Why are you here under assumed names?"

I think I'm pretty much done answering questions.

"Assumed names?" Georgie affects a look of innocent confusion.

"Your sister is registered in school as Fritzi Moore."

Boy, they really have been digging around.

"But that's my name," I say and force a light laugh. "Why do you think it's an alias?"

"Your name is Fredericka Elisabetta Teresa von Boden don Mohr of Colsteinburg," the reporter pronounces carefully.

"Right," I say. "Fritzi Moore. The longer version wouldn't fit on the forms."

The cameraman laughs, and even the reporter smiles a bit.

"Why didn't King Frederick announce where you and your sister were?"

"That is something you'll have to ask him," Georgie says. Her façade is starting to crack.

"If you'll excuse us, we need to go." And with that, she takes me by the hand as if I'm a three-year-old and pulls me inside. Henri shuts and locks the door behind us.

Mam is sitting on the sofa, a throw pillow clutched tight in her hands. She looks alarmingly pale. Georgie, on the other hand, who a second ago was my ally, turns on me, high color in her cheeks.

"How could you?" she demands.

"I ..."

"You put us all in danger."

"I ..."

"You jeopardized everything Pap is doing to fix things."

"And what is he doing?" I find the gumption to fight back. "There's nothing about him in the news. He's giving no speeches, making no pleas. We don't even know if he's okay. Why shouldn't I do something to help?"

"And you think this will help?" Mam's voice is hard, and it startles me.

This is not the time to back down. What's done is done. I stand taller, throwing my shoulders back and trying to appear confident, even though I'm not.

"I do."

"Why?" Georgie asks.

I take a deep breath. If they would give me a chance to explain, maybe I could convince them.

"Soda commercials," I say, which maybe isn't the clearest way to begin.

"What?" All three of them look at me like I'm crazy.

"TV commercials make people love their products. Like soda. Everyone loves soda."

"Except maybe people who want to be healthy," Georgie says and gives me a small smile. Maybe she isn't as mad at me as I thought.

"Almost everyone, then," I say. "Anyway, how do they convince everyone to like their particular brand of soda? There are ads that show everyone being happy and loving and topping it off with their drink. So I thought I'd do the the same thing and be happy and loving and they would think happy thoughts and want us back."

Henri bursts out laughing.

I don't think it's funny; I still think it's a brilliant idea.

The tension is broken, and Georgie says, "There's a certain logic there. But why didn't you come to us? We could have at least showed you how to turn off the geo-tagging."

"You were too sad about Etienne," I say. "And I didn't even know geo-tagging was a thing."

"They found us," Mam says, her voice barely above a whisper.

"Maybe that's a good thing," I say. "If you're worried about us being hurt, we're probably safer if the whole world knows where we are and is watching. Who's going to hurt us if a TV camera is filming?"

Mam stands up, and for the first time since we've left home, she almost looks regal. "Someone who wants the world to know you've been hurt." She sweeps past me and up the stairs.

My mouth goes dry.

"Why would someone want the world to know that?" I ask Georgie.

She has her arms crossed in front of her, and her face is ashen.

"I don't know."

That does not make me feel any better. Georgie is supposed to have the answers.

"No one will hurt you," Henri assures us.

I curl up on the sofa and try to figure this out. How would it help anyone if people knew they had hurt us? Would it make someone like them more? Of course not; Georgie and I are innocent girls. No one wants to see us hurt. People might want a different government, but I can't believe they'd really want to see something bad happen to the royal family. Visions of the execution of the Romanov family over a hundred years ago flash through my mind. But that was a long time ago, and things were different then. And for what it's worth, the Romanov murderers didn't exactly go public with the information. No. We are definitely safer if the TV cameras are following us around than if they aren't.

I check my phone to see how many views my video has gotten since I'd been at school. My video has thousands of views and has been reposted all over the place. There are tons of positive comments. Some negative ones too, to be sure, but I won't let myself focus on those right now.

"We need to make another video," I say when Henri has gone into the kitchen and left us alone.

"I don't think so," Georgie says. "Look how much trouble one video caused."

"But that's because it let them find us. They already found us. So what's the harm? Besides, you need be in one with me."

She shakes her head, but this is one time I know what I'm talking about.

"What this fight needs is more positive publicity."

Georgie raises one eyebrow and waits for me to continue, looking at me over the rising steam in her cup.

"Our side is not getting the word out. But we can," I say. "People liked my video yesterday. People are talking about it."

"And what would you say in your next video?" Georgie challenges me.

"We tell people where we are."

Georgie frowns.

I point out the window. "They've figured it out already, but if we make a video, announcing it, then we can't be portrayed as hiding anything."

"Maybe," Georgie says, drawing out the word like she's not really convinced yet.

"You're next in line for the throne. People have to know you haven't abandoned them. It's very important." I pause, and she doesn't say no, so I'm going to assume that she'll do it.

"Should I turn off the geo-tagging?" I ask as I get out my phone.

"Doesn't really matter at this point," Georgie says, "if we're going to tell them where we are anyway. And I know just what to say."

I smile. I like being a team with Georgie.

We sit on the sofa, and I hold the phone out at arm's length and start the video.

"*Hallo!*" I start like I did last time. "Prinzessin Fredericka here."

"And Prinzessin Georgiana," Georgie adds. "We are in Boston," she says. "We came for the chowder, which is so good we thought we would stay awhile. But we'll be home soon. We love you all and miss you!"

"*Prost!*" I say and end the video.

"That's all there is to it?" Georgie asks.

"Short and sweet, that's my theory. More people are apt to watch it if it's short."

I upload it, share it, and cross my fingers that this all works out like we hope.

CHAPTER 15

Wednesday morning, I get dressed for school, wishing I had something other than jeans and T-shirts to wear. Everyone knows I'm a princess now, and I'd like to look like one. Of course, my grandmother would tell me that it's not the clothes we wear that make us who we are, but how we act. Finally, I can act like a princess again. I'm actually looking forward to going to school.

When I get down to breakfast, there are boxes of cereal on the table, and Georgie and Mam are deep in conversation with Henri. They all look up when I enter, and I know they were talking about me, though I can't imagine what the issue is. I'm up and dressed and ready for school, and I'm not giving anyone any attitude.

I pick up a box of cereal and prepare to pour some into a bowl.

"You are not going to school today," Henri says.

I put the box down, bowl still empty, and look at the three of them. Mam, as is often the case these days, looks slightly shell-shocked. Henri looks grim and determined, but it's Georgie's face that worries me. She is pale, and there is a hint of fear in her eyes that I don't like at all.

"Why? What happened?" I ask. "Is it because the reporters know where we are?"

"It's because we've had death threats against Georgiana," Henri says.

Mam gets up and walks out of the kitchen without a word.

"Death threats?" I'm glad I didn't pour the cereal. I'm not hungry any more.

"I'm sure it's nothing," Georgie says, false bravado in her voice. "I mean, just someone trying to scare me."

"Is it working?" I ask.

"Of course not," Georgie says and forces a laugh so I'll believe her. I don't.

"Well, it scares me," I say.

"It scares me as well," Henri says. "I cannot protect the three of you if you are not all in the same place. I must insist you stay home today. Besides, there are still news vans outside hoping to catch a glimpse of the royal family. It is better if we do not give them more to talk about."

"Oh." I don't argue with him. There are plenty of things to fight about, and being allowed to go to a school I don't like that much isn't really one of them. "What kind of threats?" I ask.

“The kind is not important,” Henri says.

We’ve had death threats against us before. Usually, what happens is that we are kept under tight security at the palace for about a week or so until the threat has been neutralized. That’s how they always word it. “The threat has been neutralized.” I’m not stupid, though. I know it means that a team of investigators and police and whoever else Pap has at his disposal, which is pretty much everyone in the kingdom, has done mountains of work to find and arrest the person who made the threat. All we have is Henri. What can he do except not let us go out? That won’t neutralize anything. We’ll be prisoners here as effectively as if someone else had actually taken us prisoner.

“I’m sure it’s nothing to worry about,” Georgie says. “Just someone who wants to feel important by making threats. A big bully. That is all.”

“It doesn’t have anything to do with the coup?” I ask, skeptical.

“Impossible to say,” Henri says. He gets up and pours himself more coffee. “But I will keep you safe. I assure you.”

“So, what are we going to do all day?” I ask. “Just hide out in here?”

It turns out that’s exactly what we end up doing. The townhouse is small; there’s no getting away from everyone. By lunchtime, the last of the news vans have given up, and I’ve watched all the cat videos I can stand. I want to be back at the palace. I want to be in the palace gardens, where there are acres to roam without any danger at all. There is a swing in a huge maple tree, and I could swing and marvel at the changing colors of the leaves. That's where I want to be right now.

I'm so bored I wish I had fought to be allowed to go to school.

As a special lunch treat, Henri makes meat and cheese rolls like we eat at home, but the cheese doesn't taste right, and it only makes me wish even harder that I was back in Colsteinburg and everything was as it should be.

"What do you think is going on at home?" I ask. "Do you think Pap is okay?"

Mam gets up from the table and walks to the window, not even glancing my way. Georgie takes a deep breath but doesn't really follow it up with anything. I look at Henri, and he hesitates before meeting my eye.

"It's very hard to know."

"But if something really bad happened, we would know, right? I mean, no news is good news and all that." No one answers me. I push my plate away, no longer the least bit hungry. I need to find out what's going on at home.

I run upstairs. If something really bad had happened, of course we would know about it. If he were dead or had abdicated, it would be all over the news. If we haven't heard anything, it's because he's still plotting his strategy; that has to be the answer. But just to be sure, I pull out my tablet and search for him. Maybe there is an answer out there if we look hard enough.

What I find are lots of people with opinions. Some people still back the monarchy, but they are drowned out by the opposition.

More than once, I see Pap referred to as a playboy, a dilettante, or a pretty boy, but that doesn't make sense. Pap is a dedicated family man and so in love with Mam that the thought of him having an affair is absolutely laughable.

Georgie walks into the bedroom we share.

"Are you okay?" she asks.

"What's a dilettante?" I ask her, ignoring her question. I'm not okay, and we both know it.

She sits on the bed next to me. "An amateur, I think."

"Why would people call Pap an amateur? Because he hasn't been king long?"

"Because people think he's just playing at it, that he doesn't really want to be king."

"Of course he wants to be king," I say.

Georgie doesn't answer right away.

"He does want to be king, right?" I persist.

"I think he wasn't quite ready for Grandpa to die so soon. He thought he'd have more time before he had all the responsibility."

If that's all it was, we all thought that. Who thought after King Franz lived into his nineties that King George would die when he was only in his sixties? No one was ready for Pap to have to take over, but that is no reason for a coup. That's simply a reason to give him a chance.

"And why would they call him a playboy?" I ask. "Do they think he would cheat on Mam? Because he wouldn't, and you better not tell me he would."

"Of course he wouldn't," Georgie says. "I think they mean he likes to party and have fun. They're trying to make Orcutt seem like the serious one and Pap seem unfit."

"But they're lying," I say. "We can't let them get away with lying like that."

"You don't understand," Georgie says.

I jump up from the bed. "I'm tired of people telling me I don't understand. If people would take the time to explain it to me, I would. I'm not an idiot, you know." I take a deep breath. "I'm going out."

"Where do you think you're going?" Georgie asks in a way that sounds very much like Mademoiselle Colette or the headmistress at school.

"Out." I repeat. "I can't stand being cooped up any longer."

"You can't," Georgie says. "Henri wants us to stay in."

"I don't care," I say. "I need to get out."

"I don't want you to."

"I'll be gone ten minutes tops. I just need to get out of the house." I don't give her a chance to respond. I rush down the stairs and step outside. I feel like I'm making a daring escape from prison or something, but all I'm doing is going for a walk.

I probably have three minutes before Henri comes after me. I don't care. It's freedom.

I walk fast, not caring where I'm going, just trying to give myself more of a head start over Henri.

Pap a dilettante? An amateur? A playboy? That is not who

Pap is, not even a little. Why can't people see Pap the way I see him? Maybe they can! All I need to do is film more videos and tell them.

I've walked to the school, which wasn't my plan, but it isn't really surprising considering it's the only place in town I've been so far. I check my watch. Classes will get out soon. It's quiet and peaceful here, but that will change in a few minutes. I sit on the brick steps, warm from the afternoon sun, to film my video.

"*Hallo,* Prinzessin Fredericka here. When King George died, my father, even in his sorrow, was thinking of Colsteinburg. 'May God grant me the wisdom and strength to rule as wisely as those who came before me.' That's what he said. He loves Colsteinburg. We all do. *Prost!*"

I upload the video. I'll have to make more. I can share favorite memories of Pap, let people see what he's like as a father. I'm sure I can convince them to all love him as much as I do, if they'll only listen. Right now, I'd better move on. I don't want to find myself in the middle of a crowd when the school bell rings. I may have escaped from Henri temporarily, but then again, that means I don't have any security, and even though the death threat was against Georgie, that doesn't mean I'm in the clear. I know better than to take unnecessary risks.

When I stand, I find myself face to face with a stranger. He is medium height and weight, wearing jeans and a green polo shirt. His goatee is the only thing that might set him apart from anyone else. I let out a startled squeak and take a step backwards as my heart beats double-time.

I never should have left the safety of the townhouse. Now I'm going to be murdered here on the school steps, and Georgie will never forgive me.

CHAPTER 16

The stranger reaches out to steady me. "Do not be afraid, Your Royal Highness." He speaks to me in German, the language of home, and I start to relax. "I am Felix Martel. A friend of your father's. May I speak with you?"

A friend of Pap's. I'm not about to be murdered. Instead, I've found help. I breathe a sigh of relief.

"Is Pap all right? Have you seen him?"

"I have. Let us walk and talk. I do not want to arouse suspicion."

I walk with him in the opposite direction from our townhouse, heading to a part of town I have yet to explore, but I feel safe. He is a friend of Pap's.

"Tell me," I say, bouncing a little as I walk. "What has Pap said to you? Is he coming here? Does he want us to go home?"

"Hold on, little one," Felix says. "Your father does not want you to go home yet. Things are still too unstable, but he did send me a gift to bring you." He hands me the canvas bag he is carrying.

"What is it?" I ask, even as I open the bag and see Sir Fred, my old teddy bear, nestled inside. I pull him out and hold him close. No, I haven't needed him since I was five, but boy is it nice to have this comforting bit of home back in my arms. "Pap sent this to me? You've seen him? He's okay?"

"Things are not easy for him, Your Royal Highness. He misses you and your mother and sister."

"Then we should go to him," I say. All I want is to be home and back with Pap again.

"*Nein.* It is not time. Not yet."

We stop at a traffic light, and I put the bear back in the bag. I may be delighted to have him back again, but that doesn't mean I want to be seen hugging a teddy bear. I am twelve, after all.

"Come home with me," I say, thinking of how much Mam would like seeing someone from Colsteinburg. Especially one of Pap's friends. It will totally help draw her out of herself.

"*Nein.* It is better they do not know I am here."

The light changes to green, and we cross, walking into a residential area with old houses and small front lawns. It isn't really like Colsteinburg, where our houses in town are built very close together, and those in the country have lots of space around them, and they all have red tile roofs, and most have flower boxes at every window. I want to be back home.

"Why?"

"I am operating in secret. Working for your father."

"But then you should want to see my mother and Henri." Of course anyone who has any information about Pap should see Mam. That seems very clear to me.

"Henri," Felix says with a nod. "He is not so discreet as I am. He will give away my plan. It is best he not know you saw me."

"You don't trust Henri?" I ask, feeling a flutter of doubt in my heart. Henri is all that is keeping us safe. If we can't trust him, then where will we turn? Suddenly, the peaceful houses around us all might be harboring assassins waiting for me to make a mistake, like going out without security.

"To keep you safe? Yes, I trust him implicitly for that. You should have no fear. To keep a secret about my mission? That is different." He is so calm and soothing. There is really no reason not to trust what he says. After all, he brought me my bear. He must have spoken to Pap.

"What is Pap doing to end the coup?" I ask.

"It's all very complicated and taking place in diplomatic circles. I can't give any details."

I sigh in frustration. "I want to help," I say. "What can I do to help? Everyone tells me I'm too young, but I must be able to do something."

"Maybe you can help," Felix says, as if struck by sudden inspiration.

"How?"

"Your videos," Felix says.

A little glimmer of pride burns inside me. "Should I keep doing them?"

"Of course," Felix says. "But also, let your father know how much you miss him. He sees the videos and appreciates them."

"He does?" I'm helping Pap. I knew these videos were a good thing.

"But it is dangerous for him there. Many of his friends are in hiding. He needs to go someplace safe so that he can regroup and rally his friends around him."

"Shouldn't he do that in Colsteinburg?"

We get to another street. This one has no traffic light, but we don't cross it. Instead, we turn the corner and keep walking. Does Felix know where we are going, or are we just wandering? I wish he would come back home with me. Mam and Georgie can keep a secret. If Henri cannot, we simply won't tell him anything. It's as easy as that.

"Too dangerous," Felix answers me.

"But isn't the military on his side? Won't they keep him safe?"

Felix gives me a sad sort of smile. "It's very hard to know who is friend and foe right now. It would be better for him if he were to leave the country. To be somewhere safe."

"But he can't leave. If he does, he abdicates!"

"Nonsense," Felix says. "He's traveled out of the country before. It doesn't mean he's not king."

This is true. We've come to America before and of course to

France and Germany and Switzerland. Why, he probably spends almost half the year outside of Colsteinburg. I imagine Pap living with us in the townhouse, all safe and together. It would be wonderful.

"Ask him to come to you. Tell him how much you miss him. You know he would do anything for you."

Would he? I know some people say I am spoiled, but would my father put my wishes above the good of Colsteinburg? Probably not. Then again, if my wishes were also for the good of Colsteinburg—that he get to a safe place, with us, in order to strengthen his position—then I might be able to convince him.

"I can try," I say.

"That is good," he answers. "You try. But remember, this is our secret. Do not tell anyone you saw me or what my plan is. For it to work, we require total secrecy."

"Right," I say, even as I try to figure out what about this plan wouldn't work if Georgie or Mam knew about it.

"I must go," Felix says. "Remember, tell no one you saw me." And with that, he hurries off down the road, leaving me alone. I'm not even sure where I am. But groups of kids start coming toward me. School has obviously gotten out. I walk against the crowd until I get back to the school.

Once the school building is in sight, I breathe a sigh of relief. I can find my way home from here.

"Where's your entourage?"

I spin around and come face to face with Jasmine and her friends.

"I gave them the day off. It's so hard for a princess to get out by herself these days, you know." My false bravado becomes real as I speak.

Jasmine grins. "I'm sure." She scuffs her sneaker against the ground. "You weren't in school today."

"I know, Henri wouldn't let me."

"Who's Henri?"

"My mother's bodyguard."

"Where is he now?"

"I gave him the slip." I look over my shoulder. "I expect him to find me any minute."

"Huh, I had you pegged for a goody-goody."

I am a goody-goody, normally. As a princess of Colsteinburg, I can never do anything that would reflect badly on my family or the country. That pretty much keeps me in line.

"Things are not always as they seem," I answer.

"Did the news cameras finally leave you alone?"

"*Ja*, I guess they got what they needed."

Jasmine's friend, the one who reminded me of Claudia when I first saw her, studies me carefully before asking, "So, if you're really a princess, are you, like, going to be queen someday or something?"

"No, that would be my sister."

The other girl, her black hair hanging long and straight down her back, narrows her eyes and smiles. "You ever want to off her so you can be queen instead?" she asks.

I give her a withering stare, the kind my mother uses when

someone is being particularly offensive.

"Only when she gets on my nerves," I say. "Kind of like you are doing right now."

The girl takes a step back, as if she actually thinks I might strike her down. What kind of power does she think princesses have? I suspect she's watched too many animated movies. Maybe she thinks I am going to summon a legion of lethal squirrels or something. I suppress a grin at the thought.

"Marly," Jasmine says with an exasperated sigh, "you are an idiot."

"I thought we didn't like her." Marly looks confused.

Jasmine pushes her aside. "Don't listen to her," she says to me.

"She's right, though. You don't like me," I say.

Jasmine starts to deny it. I can practically see her mouth forming the words, but then she changes her mind. She crosses her arms and taps her foot as she figures out what to say.

"It's okay," I continue. "I didn't much like you either. Especially after you dumped your food on me. Nothing like a head full of pasta to make the new girl feel welcome."

Jasmine looks like she might be about to apologize but stops. Apologies probably don't come that easy to her.

"I like you better now, though," I say. "You're a decent basketball player."

Her eyes open wide. "Decent? I'm the best!"

I shrug. "If you say so."

"What's your story?" Jasmine asks suddenly. "I don't

understand you."

"Why should you?" I answer. "I bet you never met anyone like me before."

Jasmine looks momentarily amused. "That's true enough."

It is then that Henri catches up with me, and I am not at all unhappy to see him. "I must insist you return to the townhouse, Your Royal Highness," he says.

I'm not going to argue. The encounter with Felix left me jittery, and although sparring with Jasmine perked me up, I want to be behind doors, safe and secure.

"I have to go," I say to Jasmine and her friends.

"Will you be back in school tomorrow?" Jasmine asks.

I glance at Henri before answering.

"Probably," I say.

"It is unlikely," he says.

We'll negotiate that later, but if I have to stay trapped in the townhouse for too much longer, I'll go crazy.

"Well, maybe we'll see you then," Jasmine says, and they head off in one direction while I let Henri escort me back home.

"I don't suppose I have to tell you how dangerous going off on your own is," he says.

"Nothing happened to me," I say. I'm itching to tell him about Felix but don't.

"What's that you have there?" Henri asks, eyeing the bag I'm carrying.

"Oh this?" I can't tell him, can I? I can't tell anyone I have Sir

Fred back, because then I'd have to tell them how I got him, and I can't give away Felix's secret. "It's just something Jasmine gave me. It has to do with a project I was supposed to do in school today." I don't like lying, but what choice do I have?

Back home, Georgie is pacing the floor and turns on me when I come in with Henri. "Where did you go? Anything could have happened to you! You can't just go about unescorted! If you don't do that at home, where everyone knows you and you know your way around, why would you think you can do that here?"

"I'm sorry," I say, really feeling bad now that I see how upset Georgie is. "Nothing happened to me. I'm fine. You don't have to worry."

"Of course I have to worry. It's not like I have anything else to do."

This, unfortunately, is true.

Henri has melted away into the kitchen, leaving me alone with Georgie. "I really am sorry," I say. "I just needed to get out."

"You're not the only one who feels trapped here," Georgie says. "At least you go out most days to school."

She's right, and now I feel even worse.

"Do you think Pap has enough friends on his side back home?"

Georgie takes a deep breath, and I see tears pooling in her eyes. "I don't know, Fritzi. How am I supposed to know something like that?"

"But you know everything!"

"Ha!" She stands and strides across the room, only to turn and come right back. “Know everything, do I? I don’t know how to help Mam. I don’t know what’s happening at home. I don’t know if I’m supposed to help Pap. After all, I’m the next in line. Right? I mean, this is my kingdom. My destiny. My whole life being fought over in the streets, and where am I? In a stupid tiny townhouse watching game show reruns and eating soup out of cans. Know everything?” Her voice rises in volume and pitch. “I don’t even know how to get you to obey me.” She runs upstairs, and seconds later, the door to our room slams shut.

I stay on the sofa, clutching my canvas bag. Now what?

Upstairs, a door opens, and I hear tentative footsteps on the stairs. I hope it’s Georgie, but it’s Mam who comes into view.

“Why did you slam the door, Fritzi?”

“It wasn’t me.” Nothing like being typecast as the moody and volatile one in the house. “It was Georgie.”

“Why?” Mam asks. “What did you do to her?”

“Me?” Maybe my expression of innocence might be a bit exaggerated. “I didn’t do anything. She’s cracking under the pressure. We all are. Can’t we do anything?”

“We can try to make life easier for each other. Can you manage that?”

I don’t think I’ve been making life so difficult, but I don’t bother saying that. It wouldn’t end well if I did.

“Yes, Mam,” I say. “Can we go home and help make life easier for Pap?”

The look Mam gives me is full of regal reproach. “We can help

Pap by staying here. Don't bother me with that again." She goes back to her room, and I'm left sitting on the sofa, hugging a bag that holds my teddy bear and wishing that this nightmare was over.

CHAPTER 17

When I went away to school last month, I was afraid I'd be homesick. I envisioned myself on the phone to my parents or Georgie every couple of hours, but that's not how things played out. My roommates, Sophia and Claudia, quickly became my substitute family. Sophia, of course, I'd known for years. But even in just a month, Claudia was as close to me as another sister. And now I can't be in touch with them. Even worse, Sophia has cut me off. Now I'm feeling the homesickness I thought I'd feel at school. I'm homesick for my friends as well as everything else.

Maybe a video would reach them, even if nothing else did. It's worth a try.

Henri is still in the kitchen, and Mam and Georgie are upstairs. I pull out my phone.

"*Hallo,* Prinzessin Fredericka here. Home is more than just mountains and streams. It is friends. I miss my friends, Claudia, Sophia, and everyone. I hope to see you soon. *Prost!*"

I upload the video and check the comments on some of the other ones. They've been viewed or shared hundreds of thousands of times. #PrinzessinFredericka is even trending. Maybe I really can make a difference with the videos.

I pull Sir Fred out of the bag and hold him close, tears coming to my eyes. Pap gave this to Felix to give to me. Pap is thinking about me and worrying that I'm missing my teddy bear, even with everything else he has to worry about. With the videos, I really do have the power to reach him, to help him. Felix is right that Pap should be here with us. He should be someplace where he doesn't have to worry about his physical safety so he can concern himself with winning back the country.

Pap isn't in the habit of taking advice from me, but I suppose it doesn't hurt to try. If I don't sound like a whiny kid, but instead like someone who has thought this out carefully, maybe it will be better received. I stick my bear back in the bag. Having my teddy bear by my side would not make me look like a reasoned, thoughtful, mature person.

There is no sound from upstairs. In the kitchen, I hear Henri running water. I have to assume he'll be in there at least long enough for me to make one more video.

I take a deep breath and start.

"*Hallo,* Prinzessin Fredericka here. This message is for my pap. It is not safe for you there. Come here, with us, to regroup and save the country. Colsteinburg needs you, but so do we. I miss you. *Ich leibe dich*." This video I end with "I love you" instead of "cheers." It seems more appropriate.

I upload the video.

The doorbell rings, and I jump. Is it Felix? Did he decide to come here and see Mam after all? Is it a news crew? Is it the person who threatened Georgie? I can't make myself get up and answer the door. Luckily, I don't have to. Henri is already striding to the door.

He opens it, and I am very relieved to see Mister Hart on the other side.

He nods to Henri. "Mr. Behr, nice to see you again. May I come in and speak to Her Majesty?"

"Of course," Henri says and moves aside.

The two men notice me curled up on the sofa.

"Your Royal Highness," Henri says, "You remember Ambassador Thomas Hart, don't you?"

I stand and smile and nod. "Of course," I say, holding my hand out to him. "It's a pleasure to see you again." Why is he here? Is it because of the threat against Georgie? Because of the reporters? Is he going to tell me and Georgie we shouldn't have spoken to them? Does he have news from home? Is it bad news?

"The pleasure is mine, Fredericka," he says, taking my hand.

Henri goes upstairs to get Mam and Georgie, leaving me alone with the ambassador for a moment. I want to ask him all kinds of questions about home, but he probably has things he wants to tell all of us together.

"How are you finding your temporary home?" he asks.

"It's very nice," I say. "Thank you again for letting us use it."

Before he can answer, Mam and Georgie come downstairs, and Mam greats Ambassador Hart like the old friend he is. Soon we are all sitting around the living room, waiting for whatever it is Mr. Hart came here to tell us.

He clears his throat and frowns. He does not look like a person who has good news to share. "Things are very unsettled right now. I spoke with Ivan Frank. He's lost touch with His Majesty."

Lost touch with? What does that mean? I grab Georgie's hand.

"Do they know where he is?" Georgie asks.

"Not at the present time, no."

"How can you just lose a king?" I ask.

Georgie squeezes my hand.

Mr. Hart shakes his head sadly. "I do not know what's going on over there. The reports we are getting are very contradictory."

"Do you think Frederick is still alive?" Mam asks, her voice surprisingly controlled.

Mr. Hart nods. "Yes, Your Majesty, I do. If he were not, the other side would be quick to use that to their advantage."

"We need to go home!" I say. "We need to find Pap!"

Georgie puts her free hand on my knee. "We can't help him. We need to let others do that." I don't see why. Except that others have training and experience and equipment and things like that.

Mam is sitting straight and regal in the armchair, her hands folded in her lap. She almost looks a little like her old self.

"Is there anything we can do to help Frederick?" she asks.

Mr. Hart tugs at his tie and clears his throat again. "Until he gets in touch with us, Your Majesty, we won't know what kind of help he needs."

"But you're looking for him? Right?" I ask. "I mean, someone is."

"Yes, Your Royal Highness, someone is."

"And what about the reporters?" Mam asks. "Our hiding spot has been compromised. What should we do? Should we find a new place to stay?"

"I'm working on it. It may take a few days." He turns to Henri. "Can you keep this place secure until then?"

Henri nods. "It is under control."

Henri's notion of keeping us safe is keeping us locked up. We didn't flee from our home to be prisoners, did we? What if Felix is right and Henri can't be trusted? Then what? And how is any of this helping Pap? I can't even ask these questions. I need to get away, but there's nowhere I'm allowed to go. I run upstairs. They don't need me at their little meeting anyway; I'm just a kid. I throw myself on the bed I share with Georgie and swallow hard a couple of times to keep from crying. Crying will not help.

So what can I do?

Not much. But I can make another video.

I check myself in the mirror and decide I look respectable enough. I take a deep breath and turn the camera back on.

"*Hallo!* Prinzessin Fredericka here. I love you all, and I love Colsteinburg. I also love my father, King Frederick. If anyone has seen him, please let me know. We are worried about his safety. *Danke.*"

I don't end with "*Prost*" this time. "Cheers" doesn't seem like a good way to conclude this video.

I upload the video and share it, and this time I stay online to see if there are any responses.

The responses start almost right away, but no one has seen Pap.

Everyone is real apologetic and hopes we track him down soon. They all sound concerned. These are not people who really want to overthrow the government, I'm sure of it. People who support the monarchy are out there; we just need to make sure they can have their voices heard.

There are a few who say hateful things, like they hope he is dead, but I try to ignore those.

The door opens, and Georgie peeks in.

"Are you all right?" she asks.

"I don't know." I show her the latest video and the responses to it. "No one has seen Pap. Do you think he's okay?"

Georgie reads the messages. "I hope so," she says.

"We should go home and find him."

She shakes her head. "You heard what Mr. Hart said. It's not safe. We'll show this to him and Henri. They have the contacts who can help Pap."

I suppose that is true, but something about the statement bothers me. "Why don't we have the contacts?" I ask. "We're the royal family. We know everyone. Or at least everyone knows us."

"What we don't know," Georgie says softly, "is who we can trust."

I shiver and try to tamp down the sick feeling that comes over me. "We can trust Ambassador Hart, right?" And what about Henri? And Felix? Can we really trust anyone other than ourselves?

"He gave us his house," Georgie says.

"But what if it's a trick?"

"I think we can trust him."

I'd feel a lot better if she hadn't added "I think" to that sentence.

"I'm scared," I admit.

"I know," Georgie says. She rubs my back, and the gentleness of the gesture almost makes me want to cry. I wait for her to tell me it will all be all right, that we just have to give it time. She doesn't say that.

"I want to go home," I whisper.

She shakes her head. "I know, but we can't. It's not safe."

"But we could do something to help. I know we can."

"We can't, Fritzi. You just have to accept that."

I am not going to accept that. I'm also not going to argue with Georgie about it. That would be particularly unproductive.

"What about Mam?" I ask. "Do we have to accept that she's disappeared into herself? Shouldn't she be home where she can get help?"

"She's doing better. Maybe everything's going to be okay if we just give it time."

But how much time will it take? How much do we have?

"You know what would make Mam better? Getting her home so she can be queen again."

Georgie nods. "You have to have patience, Fritzi."

But I'm out of patience.

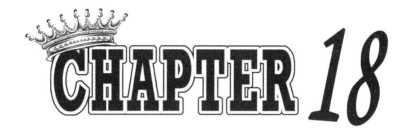

CHAPTER 18

Late at night, lying in bed next to a sleeping Georgie, I feel the worry coming back. Maybe they've lost touch with Pap because he's on his way here in response to my video. That would be good. But what if Pap doesn't see my video? What if he doesn't come? What if he can't? What if someone hurts him when he's trying to leave? Why didn't he just come here with us when he had the chance? I wish we were all together. I wish I could go home, but even if I could manage to get myself to the airport, there's no way I could either buy a ticket or convince the people at the airline that I'm allowed to travel alone.

Sometimes I wish I were as old as Georgie. Then I could do whatever I wanted.

I roll over and look at my phone. Did Pap see my video? Did

Claudia and Sophia see the one where I mentioned them? There are no messages from either of them, but Claudia has commented on the video itself with a simple "*amis pour toujours*," friends forever.

Why can't I be back at Academie Sainte Marie with her instead of here with Jasmine and Bethany, two people who are frankly a little hard to figure out? Life was easier when I was definitely a princess and got to act like it.

Though there is nothing stopping me from acting like a princess even though my country is in chaos.

I turn the camera on and hope I don't wake Georgie. There is enough light coming in the window from the street light that I think this will work.

"*Hallo!* Prinzessin Fredericka here. It is late, and I cannot sleep because my heart cries for Colsteinburg. It is my country, and I want the people there to be happy. But can't you be happy with us there as well?"

I turn off the camera and upload the video before the tears that are threatening actually come to my eyes.

"It will be all right, Fritzi," Georgie says softly.

She wasn't asleep after all. Or maybe I woke her up.

I want to answer her, but now there is a lump in my throat. None of this is fair.

She reaches out and takes me in her arms and sings a Colsteinburg lullaby to me, and finally I drift off to sleep.

When I wake up, Georgie is already out of bed. I go downstairs, where Mam is drinking a cup of coffee and Henri is scrambling eggs. "Do you want eggs, Your Royal Highness?" he asks. There doesn't seem to be any question of my going to school today.

"*Ja, bitte*," I answer and sit down at the table with Mam. "Where's Georgie?"

"She's just out on the back patio," Mam says. "Did you sleep well?"

She's beginning to sound like her old self.

"Not really," I answer.

"I haven't slept well in over week," Mam says and gazes into her coffee mug.

Over a week. It hasn't even been two weeks yet since the ball and the coup. It feels like a lifetime.

"Things will get better soon, Mam. They have to." Won't she be surprised when Pap shows up tonight and we can all work together to take back the kingdom? She'll feel so much better when she has something positive to do. I know it helped me.

Mam looks at me, and I don't like the sadness in her eyes.

"Things are not going to get better, Fritzi. I think it's time you accepted that."

"No! I will not accept that! Things will get better. Pap is taking care of everything right now. I'm sure he is." Should I tell her about Felix? Should I give her hope? Or keep the secret? I'm not sure why it has to be a secret, but Pap will come today, or tomorrow at the latest, and then I won't have to worry about it being a secret anymore. I won't say anything yet. I don't want her to be disappointed if it takes him longer than expected to get here.

Mam doesn't shrink into herself as she's done so much lately. Instead she looks intently into my eyes. "I don't think he can fix this, Fritzi."

Then I'll fix it. I don't say it out loud, though, because she would just tell me I can't, and I don't want to hear that.

Henri brings a plate with eggs and toast on it and puts it in front of me.

"You can't fix it either, Your Royal Highness," he says softly, as if he read my very thoughts.

Georgie comes in from outside. "I was talking to the boy next door," she says. "He takes classes at the local community college. Maybe I could do that, too."

"We'll see," Mam says. It sounds like she's actually considering it.

But we're going home! I want to scream. Why is everyone acting like we're staying here? I eat my eggs in silence and go back up to my room. More videos are needed. The ones I've made have gotten attention, but they haven't fixed anything yet.

It's time to get serious about that.

I dress and do my hair and try to make myself look as respectable and royal as possible. It's important that this message be just right. I pull out my notebook and flip to the last page and write down what I want to say.

When I'm ready, I turn on the camera.

"*Hallo,* Prinzessin Fredericka here! I understand that sometimes people want change. And perhaps Colsteinburg wants change too. But not everything has to change at once. Think about it. *Prost!*"

I upload it and then record another one.

"*Hallo,* Prinzessin Fredericka here! Here I see the stars and stripes of the American flag, but I long to see, once again, the dragon flag of Colsteinburg. I love my country. It is small but feisty. Kind of like me. *Prost!*"

I schedule that video to upload in an hour. In the meantime, I need to think of more short and quick things I can say.

I wish Pap had responded to the video I addressed to him. Some little note to let me know he got the message and is on the way. But I suppose I just have to take it on faith. I can't wait to see him again.

The day passes slowly. Time seems to have taken on a new dimension here, and it's driving me crazy. In the afternoon, I go down to the kitchen to see if Henri needs help.

"You did not like the meat rolls the other day?" Henri asks.

"They didn't taste like home. Almost, but not quite."

"I cannot find the right cheese here. So how about we have something American for dinner tonight?"

"Like what?"

"Spaghetti and meatballs?"

I laugh. "That's not American. That's Italian."

"Not the way I make it," Henri assures me.

Henri is no more American than the rest of us, but at least he's not mad at me for running off yesterday. I agree to help him make American spaghetti. We start with a sauce, using some from a jar and adding fresh tomatoes and peppers and onions and letting that simmer on the stove. Then we tackle the meatballs, adding a bit of any spice we can find in the cupboard to the ground beef. Henri browns them in a pan and adds them to the sauce.

"All that's left is cooking the pasta when we're ready to eat," he says.

"Do we make that from scratch?"

He holds up a box. "No, only Italians do that. This is American spaghetti." He pulls a box of pudding mix out of the cupboard and tosses it to me. "Here, you can make dessert."

It's hardly the sparkling desserts we're used to back home, but it is better than nothing.

Mam and Georgie emerge from upstairs when it's time to eat.

"We made American spaghetti," I tell them. "It's Henri's special recipe."

"This should be interesting," Georgie says, eyeing the food skeptically.

"Don't worry," I say. "I helped."

"Oh." Georgie raises her eyebrows. "I'm sure that makes everything better."

She might not think I can make everything better, but Felix said my videos were helping, and hopefully soon, my video to Pap will bring him to us. Then she'll see that I'm able to be helpful, in more than just making dinner too.

After dinner, we watch *Pirates of the Caribbean*, and it's far enough removed from our real life to offer a bit of escape. A little bit of escape, for however short a period of time, is nice.

The next day, Friday, I am still home from school but trying not to worry about it. Soon things will certainly be resolved, and I'll be back at Academie Sainte Marie. I hold on to that hope because there is so little hope to hold on to anymore.

At least we have something to look forward to today. Ambassador Hart and his wife are coming for dinner, and they're bringing the dinner.

"I wish I had something decent to wear," Mam says as she surveys the limited clothes she escaped with.

"Don't worry about it, Mam," Georgie says, putting a soothing hand on her shoulder. "The Harts know the situation. They are not expecting us to be dressed as if it were a state dinner."

"I need new clothes," Mam says with a sigh. I wish she could have new clothes, too, so she could look wonderful for Pap when he gets here.

"We could go shopping," Georgie suggests with a touch of hopefulness. Georgie loves shopping. There have been been no further threats to Georgie, and it seems likely that the initial threat was simply someone messing around. Hopefully, soon Henri will deem it safe for us to go out again.

"No!" Mam is quick to answer. "No. Not yet. Not until things settle down. It's not safe."

"We could send Henri for things," I say. After all, he bought me school supplies and gym shorts.

Mam looks at me with one eyebrow quirked. It's such a Mam look that I want to laugh. "And I can just imagine what Henri would come back with. No. I suppose I'll have to make do."

Later, as Georgie and I are getting dressed, Georgie looks at her own wardrobe with despair. "Mam is right," Georgie says. "We need new clothes."

"We could order them over the internet," I suggest.

Georgie does not look impressed.

"We're going to have to go shopping. Mam is almost her old self. Soon, maybe she won't be afraid to let us go to the mall."

Of all the things that I want to have happen soon, going to the mall is not even in the top five. I'd rather just go home and get our own things, but I know better than to suggest that.

Mr. and Mrs. Hart are dressed as casually as we are, so it doesn't feel weird to be wearing jeans. They've brought a full, traditional roast beef dinner with potatoes and salad. It's delicious, and it feels so normal to be entertaining diplomats that I almost forget that nothing is the same anymore.

At first, the conversation revolves mainly around mutual friends from the time when the Harts lived in Colsteinburg. There's no talk about the coup or danger or anything, and then Mrs. Hart, a willowy woman who matches her husband in dignity and propriety but with a gentle face, casually mentions Sophia's mother.

"I heard from Sylvia Orcutt today," she says as she butters a roll.

The wife of the leader of the opposition. Our once-upon-a-time friend.

Mam's smile looks slightly more forced than it did a moment ago.

"I hope she is doing well," she says.

"She is very sorry that this has torn apart your family. She wanted me to let you know that."

Mam nods. "Well, that's quite thoughtful of her," she says with no warmth in her voice at all.

"Cassandra, I'm so sorry things are happening the way they are, but be assured no one wants to hurt you or your family. Sylvia was very emphatic about that."

Mam sighs. "I suppose we have to be grateful for small favors."

I glance toward the door. This would be a perfect time for Pap to walk in, but the door stays resolutely shut.

"So Pap is safe? Wherever he is? No one wants to hurt him?" I ask.

The grown-ups all exchange glances, and I don't like the looks they are giving one another.

"What aren't you telling me?" I ask. "What do you know that I don't know? Is he safe?" I don't even wait for an answer, not that it looks like anyone is jumping up to reassure me. "He's got to come here. He'd be safer. He can regroup here and then get the country back!"

Mr. Hart's eyebrows jump up. "He can't do that!" he says, as if horrified by the prospect. "As soon as he leaves the country, it's as good as abdicating. As long as he stays in Colsteinburg, he has a chance of settling down the opposition."

"What?" I ask, even though I heard him perfectly well. The roast I've been eating sits like a hard lump in my belly. Did I ask him to leave only to ruin all our chances of ever getting the country back? But why would Felix tell me that if he were really on our side? He had to know this.

"He can't leave Colsteinburg," Mr. Hart repeats.

"You knew that, Fritzi," Georgie says. "He told you that when we were leaving the palace."

"But he leaves all the time. We go on vacation. He's been to America before and Paris and lots of places, and that didn't mean he stopped being king."

"It's different now," Mr. Hart says, and it's like all the air has been sucked out of the room. They're right. It is different now, and I've made a horrible mistake.

I push my chair back from the table. "May I please be excused?" I say, and without waiting for an answer, I leave my napkin by my plate and hurry from the room.

Up in my bedroom, I lock the door and take huge gulping breaths while spots dance in front of my eyes. I've ruined everything. Absolutely everything. How could I be so stupid? I sit on the floor in front of the door and put my head between my knees in an attempt not to pass out. Am I going to faint? Is that too convenient a reaction? I have to do something. I have to fix this.

My fingers shake as I pull out my phone. The first thing I do is delete the video telling Pap to come here. But it has already been viewed more than ten thousand times, and the shares are in the four digits. I can't take it back. Not that easily. Damn. Damn. Damn.

I need to make another video. I need to tell Pap not to listen to me.

I can't do that until I can breathe normally. I take a deep breath in and let it out slowly. One more time. And once more, and I think I might be able to do this. I point the camera at myself.

"Prinzessin Fredericka here. Pap. Did you see my last message? I was wrong. Don't come here. Stay where you are and save the country. We're counting on you. Please don't leave. *Ich leibe dich!*"

As soon as I finish uploading it, I grab my teddy bear. Felix lied to me. He tried to trick Pap into abdicating and used me as a pawn. And the bear. This is my bear. How did Felix get it? Did Pap really give it to him? Did Felix go into my room and take it? And what if he tampered with it in some way, put a bomb in it or a recording device?

I throw the bear across the room, afraid to have it near me.

Deep breath. Okay, maybe not a bomb. A bomb probably would have gone off by now or else I would have felt it inside the bear. But a recording device? Those could be small. Maybe he's recording everything we say. Maybe he put a GPS unit in it so he can track us if we leave the house.

I cross the room and retrieve my bear, and with the help

of a pair of nail scissors, I rip open its seams. Soon my bear is dismantled, stuffing covering the bed, but there is nothing in the bear except stuffing. He didn't do anything to Sir Fred, but I've completely destroyed him.

The doorknob rattles.

"Let me in, Fritzi," Georgie says from the other side of the door.

Feeling like I'm moving through molasses, I stand and open the door. Georgie looks at the disemboweled bear, and her mouth falls open. "What's going on?" she asks.

I shut the door behind her and relock it, then pull her over to the bed.

"I've ruined everything!" I say, and the tears start down my face.

"How could you have?" she asks, her arm around me, soothing me like I'm a child.

So I tell her about Felix and the bear and the video I made. Her arm around me stiffens, and I know she's going to yell at me and tell me how stupid I was.

"I did make a new video though. So hopefully that will help," I say.

"Oh, honey, Pap isn't going to leave Colsteinburg just because you made a video asking him to. He knows what's at stake."

I sniffle, and Georgie hands me a tissue. "Really?" I ask and wipe my nose. "Are you sure?"

She doesn't answer right away, which leads me to believe she's not entirely sure.

"If he leaves," she says finally, "it will be because he has decided that is the prudent course. It won't just be because you ask him to." She gives my shoulders a squeeze. "You're not that spoiled."

That's good to know, anyway.

"The more important thing is to figure out who Felix Martel is and what he's up to. Come downstairs. I'm sure Mam and the ambassador have some insight. They probably know him and can help sort it out."

She stands up, but I'm not quite ready to go downstairs yet. "You sure I didn't ruin everything?"

"I'm sure," she says and holds out her hand to me.

Now I have to go tell Mam what I've done. Hopefully she'll be as understanding as Georgie.

CHAPTER 19

"I can't believe Felix would betray us like that," Mam says once I've told the story. She looks ashen and has pushed her plate away. I seem to have ruined everyone's appetite, and I no longer hope to see Pap walk in that door.

It turns out that Felix was one of Pap's advisers. A friend. Or so we thought.

"Mr. Orcutt betrayed us," Georgie points out. "Why shouldn't Felix?"

"Does Frederick even know whom he can trust?" Mam asks Mr. Hart.

He looks as helpless as the rest of us and takes a gulp of his wine before answering. "There are some people who have loudly declared allegiance to one side or another, but if someone is saying one thing and meaning another, it will be a matter of trusting his instincts."

"I'm so sorry," I say for probably the hundredth time. "You don't think Pap will leave Colsteinburg, do you?"

Mam shakes her head. "No, Fritzi, I don't. And I don't blame you. Felix tricked you." The lines between her eyes deepen, and she catches me with what can only be described as a look of royal disapproval. "You should never have been out on your own though. It could have been so much worse."

I'm afraid to ask what she thought could have happened, but images of bands of assassins chasing me through the streets of town come unbidden to mind, and I shudder.

"I will keep you safe, Your Royal Highness," Henri says to me. "But you must let me do my job."

Right. I am now well and truly chastened. No more running off on my own.

"Tell me about these videos you are making," Mrs. Hart says, and although I don't want to think of the one I made urging Pap to leave, I don't mind the change of subject.

"The videos are supposed to convince the people of Colsteinburg that they still want the royal family, kind of like ads convince everyone they like soda." I pull out my phone and show some of them to her.

"Those are adorable," she says. "Very cute. Have you done any in English?"

"Why would I? Everyone in Colsteinburg speaks German." It's

true we study English and French in school, but there's no point in doing the videos in all those languages.

"Yes, but people in America speak English."

I must look particularly blank because she goes on to explain.

"Americans love an underdog," Mrs. Hart says, a huge smile on her face.

"Underdog?" I look to Georgie for clarification.

"Someone who is almost certain to lose. Someone whom all the odds are against."

Underdog. We are the royal family. We are not people who get sympathy by being thought of as losers. "The videos are not designed to make people feel sorry for losers," I say, a hard edge to my voice that I don't even recognize. "They are to rally the people of Colsteinburg. I do not need American pity."

Mam looks horrified that I would use such a tone, but I don't care. It's past the time to worry about protocol and etiquette. Georgie has sympathy in her eyes, as if she knows something that I haven't accepted yet. Well, I will not accept our loss if that's what it's all about. Henri is staring at his food, not even making eye contact with me. Mrs. Hart looks surprised by my reaction, but also almost pitying, as if I really am an underdog in need of sympathy.

Ambassador Hart is a true diplomat, and his expression is impossible to read. He's the one who answers me.

"Your Royal Highness," he says, with no hint of condescension at all. "You must understand, from here it is very difficult to get a full reading on the hearts and minds of the people of Colsteinburg. But do not underestimate the power of having the American press and the American people behind you. Trust me, that would be a good thing."

Georgie nods encouragingly, and I swallow the hurt that comes with the term underdog. Fine.

"How is this good?" I ask.

Mr. Hart puts down his fork and gives me his full attention, "If public opinion is on your side, you are more likely to get the politicians to step up and do the right thing. Perhaps we'd even be able to get you State Department security. Perhaps they would send someone to help Frederick negotiate a truce with the opposition. What the American people like gets noticed."

"I guess I can do some in English if that would help."

"I think it would," Mrs. Hart says and gives me a warm smile, which does help make me feel a bit better about everything that's going on.

"I don't know," Mam says, "Perhaps you shouldn't do any more videos." The good feeling starts to dissipate.

"No," Mr. Hart says thoughtfully. "Let her keep doing them. They are doing no harm, and like I said, they may be helpful."

"They are undignified," Mam says.

"So is running away," I answer.

There is an awkward silence around the table, and then Mr. Hart starts talking about the weather, and Mrs. Hart asks about dessert and goes out to the kitchen for the pastries they brought.

I barely touch my strawberry tart, and I don't say anything else the rest of the night.

As we get ready for bed, Georgie chastises me. "You don't have to make things harder for everyone. It wasn't Mam's idea to run away. Why make her feel bad?"

"I wasn't trying to make Mam feel bad." I slump down onto the bed. "I just hate this whole situation, and it doesn't feel like anyone is doing anything to make it better except my videos, and Mam thinks they're undignified? Well, I'd rather be undignified and win than dignified and lose."

"We might not win," Georgie says.

"We have to win." I get into bed and turn away from her. I don't want to discuss this anymore, and I don't want her to contradict me.

Over the weekend, I make a couple of the videos over again in English and watch as the number of views skyrockets. I don't know if it will really help, but people are watching and talking about them. I don't make over the one asking Pap to come to America. That one is better left forgotten.

We hear nothing from him. He doesn't show up at the front door, and there is no message from him on any of the videos. There is no phone call. No text message. Nothing. Where is he? Did Felix really see him? How much of what he said was a lie?

If I never see Felix again, it would be too soon.

But what if he wasn't lying? He was Pap's trusted adviser. Maybe he did know what he was talking about. How do we know that what Ambassador Hart said about Pap effectively abdicating if he left the country is true? Rulers leave countries all the time, and it doesn't mean they stop being the ruler. Maybe Ambassador Hart is wrong. Maybe it would be better for Pap to be here.

How could I even ever find out?

I wish I really knew what was going on and what was the best thing to do.

It's funny. I read my history books, and everything seems so straightforward. Of course this action led to this result, what else could it have done? What the history books don't talk about are all the actions not taken and what results those might have led to.

I want to ask Mam or Georgie, but Georgie has on headphones and is busy with calculus problems, and Mam is curled up on the sofa with a thick book. Neither of them looks much like they want to be interrupted.

History books also skip over all the long, boring parts filled with waiting for something to happen. I wish I could skip those parts too. Though maybe if the ending isn't going to be good, I don't want to rush it.

A few news vans ride up and down the street a couple of times, but we don't go out, and there's nothing for them to see, so they eventually go away.

I can't take another day like this.

When we all sit down for dinner, I take a deep breath and just say what I need to say.

"I want to go back to school tomorrow."

"No," Mam says without even thinking about it. "It's not safe."

"How is it any more dangerous than sitting in the townhouse?"

"Anyone could get you there."

"No," I contradict. "The doors are locked, and there is a security guard at the door. Anyone who gets there after school opens has to ring the doorbell to get in, show ID to the security guard, and then sign in at the main office. It's very safe."

I've not only been observing things, I also spent a little time online to find the security setup at the school. "All Henri has to do is go to the office and tell them the people who should not be allowed in, like Felix, and also to call him if anyone wants to go into one of the classes I'm in."

Mam is still shaking her head.

"I'm going crazy, Mam," I start to plead. "I need to be doing something other than sitting around here. I'm a kid. I should be in school. I need to learn things and be with kids my age. I need to have something to think about other than what's going on at home."

"She's right," Georgie says. "And there have been no more threats. The media attention has died down, and if Henri brings her back and forth to school and no one can get in, then how could there be a problem?"

Mam shakes her head, but she's wavering.

"What do you think, Henri?" I ask. "Would it be safe for me?"

"Obviously, I would prefer to have all three of you in the same place, but as you say, the security at the school is such that it should not be a problem. If it is all right with Her Majesty, I will undertake the necessary measures to see that you are safe at the school starting tomorrow."

I look back at Mam. It's all up to her. She hasn't made a decision in almost two weeks. If she's going to start asserting her authority again, I sure hope she comes down in my favor on this one.

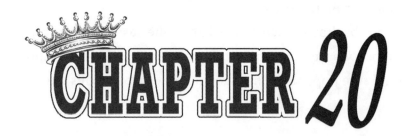

CHAPTER 20

It's Monday morning, and I'm sitting in Spanish class as if it's the most natural thing in the world. Mam actually agreed to let me go, though I think mainly she wanted me out from underfoot at the townhouse.

I take out my Spanish notebook and smile at Bethany, who is sitting next to me. "Did you have a good weekend?" I ask.

Bethany looks at me through narrowed eyes. "You weren't in school most of last week," she says, as if lobbing an accusation at me.

"I know. Henri didn't think it was safe."

"Who's Henri? Is he the man who picked you up the other day? Is he your mother's lover or something?" There's a sarcastic edge to Bethany's voice that I don't remember from last week.

"No!" I'm so shocked by the question that I almost shout. "My mother's lover? What a thing to say! He's her bodyguard. And he didn't think it was safe."

"Some bodyguard if he couldn't even keep you safe around here." She waves her hand to indicate the classroom and I suppose by extension the neighborhood.

"That's not the point," I say. This is a ridiculous conversation.

"Yeah, well. You can't just come to school whenever you want, you know. I mean, it's a waste of the teacher's time if you don't really mean to be there."

"The teacher has to be here anyway," Jasmine says, with barely a glance at Bethany as she walks past our desks to one in the back.

The tension in my shoulders eases a little at this support from an unexpected corner. I want to say something to Jasmine, to thank her or at least acknowledge that I appreciate her words, but she's not looking at me as she takes her seat. Next to me, Bethany stares at her desk, her cheeks bright red. Do a few words from Jasmine really make her feel that awful?

Jasmine really is the queen bee in this school. It's a good thing she seems to have decided to be on my side. But why has Bethany turned on me? What did I do to earn that animosity? Skip school? Or is it because I wasn't honest with her before? Maybe I'll sit with her at lunch today and try to explain. I wish I were back at my own school with Claudia and Sophia. But no. Even my best friend has turned on me in all of this. Life is so unfair.

Señora Sanchez starts class, and I think about translations and conjugations for awhile. When class ends, Bethany doesn't even look at me as she bolts from the room. I gather my books together and look for Jasmine, but she is chatting with Marly and her other friend, Jordan, and doesn't notice me.

I head to math class on my own. I guess I'm the girl without friends this week. I'll have to do something about that.

Later, as I change for gym, a girl whose name I don't know looks at me and rolls her eyes. "If you're a princess, then how come your shorts come from Walmart?"

I'm not sure what one has to do with the other, and I stare at her for a second before answering. "The princess store was all out. This was the next best option." The girl doesn't look convinced by my answer. "You know," I continue conversationally, "there isn't a dress code for being a princess."

"There should be," she says, trying for high and mighty and sounding petulant instead.

"I'll let the queen know you think so. I'm sure she'll really value your opinion."

The girl isn't sure how to respond to that, so she tosses her flat-ironed hair over her shoulder and walks away from me.

Yeah. Whatever.

Once again, when teams are chosen for basketball, I'm on Jasmine's.

She nods at me without speaking as I join her on the gym floor. I nod back. Somehow we've managed to come to a truce. That is much better than outright hostilities.

"Woo!" another girl shouts. "We have the princess."

And that's when I realize that people who never even bothered to learn my name last week are all calling me "princess."

I am a princess, but the way everyone throws the term around so casually as if it were my name and not my title is a little uncomfortable. No one here seems to know anything about the proper way to address a member of the royal family or even how to use a title properly. At least they recognize me for who I am. That counts for something.

Our team wins, and Jasmine high-fives me, still without speaking. Bethany won't even look my way. I'm not sure coming to school is really so much better than being at home. At least there, people spoke to me.

At lunchtime, I stand with my bagged lunch, for once not certain about where I should sit. Should I try to make things up with Bethany? I glance at Bethany's table, but she's not even looking at me. Should I see if the truce Jasmine and I seem to have is strong enough to survive lunch? Maybe I should sit with people I don't know yet and make new friends? I could probably use some new friends at this school.

As I scan the lunchroom looking for a likely new group of friends, Jasmine sees me and waves me over to her table. Well, maybe it is better to build a friendship on whatever we have going than to start all over again. What could have prompted this new friendliness from Jasmine? Is it just because I'm a princess? Maybe. I can live with that. I head to the table by the window.

I sit down and open my lunch.

"Any more of that royal baloney?" Jasmine asks me, and I know she's figured out I was messing with her the other day.

"No. Today it is Imperial roast beef. The favorite sandwich meat of all the tsars of Russia."

"You're making that up, right?" Marly asks, sounding as if she really isn't sure.

"*Ja*," I say with a grin. "I'm making it up."

Across the table from me, Jasmine laughs, and suddenly the atmosphere feels relaxed and almost normal.

"Do you like have a chef and all kinds of servants and everything?" Jordan asks.

"Not here. They all stayed behind. We're staying at a friend's place. We've been living mainly on frozen dinners and takeaway."

"Let me guess," Jasmine says, "last night was Imperial roast beef?"

"Just like the tsar used to eat," I answer.

"I had to have dinner with my grandmother," Jordan says, "and then I had to wash all the dishes. You're lucky you have a maid."

"I don't—" I start, but Jasmine shakes her head.

"Don't try to explain," she says. "It's not worth it."

"I looked up your country," Marly says, picking pickles off her hamburger. "I never heard of it, but it turns out it's real."

"We just have a really elaborate website," I say. Turns out it's real, indeed.

Marly's eyes widen as if she actually believes me.

"I'm kidding," I assure her. "Our country is real."

"Marly," Jasmine says with an over-elaborate sigh, "stop being an idiot." She looks at me over her bottle of water. "Things are pretty messed up there now, though."

I close my eyes until the urge to cry leaves. "Really messed up," I say finally.

"What's the deal with the videos?" Jasmine asks. "I mean, I saw them, and they're cute, but only some of them are in English. Spanish I can handle, since my grandma makes me watch her 'stories' with her whenever I'm over, but whatever that is you're speaking, I don't understand."

"German," I say. "And mostly, the English ones are just translations of the German ones."

"Ah. The only thing I knew for certain from the German ones is that you apparently like soda."

"Have you ever seen their commercials?" I ask, knowing full well she has. Everyone has; that's why I used them as a guide.

"Sure," she answers.

"I love them!" Marly says, her eyes wide. "Were you in an ad?"

I cock my head and look at her, trying to figure out what she's talking about.

"Shut up, Marly," Jasmine says and turns back to me. "Okay, so commercials."

"Right. They're short and sweet and make everyone want to drink more soda. So I wanted to make videos that were short and sweet and made everyone want the royal family back."

"Aww!" Jordan presses one hand to her heart. "That is so

sweet. Such a great idea. Is it working?"

"I don't know," I admit. "People are watching them, but I don't know if it's going to save the kingdom."

"Saving the kingdom is a pretty tall order," Jasmine says.

"But it's what I want," I say, trying not to sound petulant.

"And as princess, you're used to getting what you want?" Jasmine asks, one eyebrow quirked.

"Well, yeah," I admit, though the way she says it, it sounds like maybe I am a bit spoiled after all.

"Can I see one of the videos?" Jordan asks.

Jasmine pulls out her phone and plays one of the videos for Jordan and Marly to see. It's one of the German ones.

"So, what are you saying there?" Jasmine asks.

"That I miss my country and that my country might be small, but it is feisty, kind of like me."

Jasmine grins. "Feisty. I like that. Feisty Fritzi!"

"That could totally be a hashtag!" Marly says.

"Oooh," Jordan says, taking up the idea. "We could get T-shirts and everything!"

While I love the support from this unexpected area, I'm not sure what good T-shirts would do.

"Where would we even get T-shirts?" Jasmine asks Jordan. "But a hashtag, now that could work." The next thing I know, she's taking a selfie with me. "Princess Power!" she says. "Hashtag FeistyFritzi!"

I laugh. It feels good to laugh. Nothing has seemed very funny lately. Maybe with their help, I can actually make a difference.

Across the cafeteria, Bethany is glaring at us. I stop laughing and nudge Jasmine. "What's the story with Bethany? She seemed nice when I first got here, but now she won't talk to me."

Jasmine shrugs. "Yeah. She's all about helping the underdog. But you showed her you didn't need her help. If you don't need her, she doesn't need you."

Underdog. There's that term again. "Do you think I'm an underdog?" I ask.

"You! Heck, no! You're a princess! And you don't let yourself get pushed around. I admire that."

"Princesses don't get pushed around," I explain.

"Do you go to like princess school to learn stuff like that?" Marly asks.

Before Jasmine can tell her not to be stupid, again, I answer. "Sort of. My grandmother taught me."

"Kind of like in *Princess Diaries*?" Jordan asks.

I know what she's talking about. I saw the movie where the girl discovers she's a princess and her grandmother teaches her all the ins and outs.

"Not exactly. I mean, I always knew I was a princess, so it was stuff my sister and I learned from when we were babies."

"Will you still be a princess if the coup is successful?" Jasmine asks.

My shoulders tense again. I want to say that I will always be a princess, that that is who I am. That it can't be taken from me. But in reality, perhaps it can.

"I don't know," I say.

None of them offer any snappy comebacks to that, for which I am both grateful and sorry. I wish one of them would have said that of course I'll always be a princess. I'd like someone to think it, other than myself.

In the awkward silence that has descended on the table, I shift the subject back to underdogs. I need to understand this phenomenon.

"Do people like underdogs better than other people?" I ask. That seems to be what Mrs. Hart thought.

"Losers do," Jasmine answers dismissively.

"I don't know," Jordan says. "I think people do. They like rooting for the person who seems to have the odds against them."

"But," I muse, "if you need people on your side to win, and people only back the one who is losing, how do you ever win and have people like you?"

"Some people like winners," Marly says helpfully.

"Not Bethany," I answer. "Are there a lot like her?"

"Enough," Jasmine says. "You're thinking about your country?"

"*Ja*," I say. "I want the videos to convince people to back the king, and the other day someone told me they could be helpful because the American people like the underdog. But you are saying that if you start winning, people stop supporting you."

"I don't know if that's always true. People like the underdog to win," Marly says.

"But what about the next time? Then he's not an underdog. Is he allowed to win again?" This is all so confusing.

"You only have to win once," Jasmine points out. "Just long enough to get the country back."

This is a very good point.

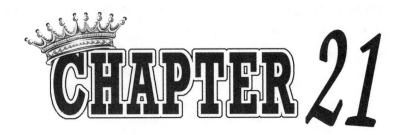

CHAPTER 21

"Are you going to the student-teacher volleyball game?" Jasmine asks as I stand at my locker, staring at my things, trying to remember what books I need to bring home.

"I don't think so," I say. I've seen posters for it, but I don't know the teachers or most of the students, and besides, it costs three dollars. "I don't have any spending money," I say and grab my math and Spanish books before shutting the locker.

"Is that the only reason? I'll spot you the cash. You're a princess, I'm sure you're good for it."

"Only if the coup doesn't succeed," I say with a sigh.

"Then consider it my contribution to the cause. Come on. It will be fun."

I don't exactly want to go back to the townhouse. All I have to look forward to is the claustrophobic feeling of not having anywhere else to go and the tension that comes from not knowing what is going on back home.

"I'll have to let someone know I'm not going home," I say. "Henri is probably waiting for me right now."

"Sure," Jasmine says. "I mean, if you're going to live here, they have to expect you to get involved in the school and stuff, right?"

"I'm not going to live here," I say. "We're just here until everything gets straightened out at home."

Jasmine doesn't look bothered by that. "Whatever. You're here now. You should be allowed to have fun."

This is true. If we've been removed from Colsteinburg to get us away from the coup, it follows that we're not expected simply to hunker down as if we were still home and in immediate danger. Why shouldn't I go to an after-school activity?

Henri is out front waiting for me. I hand him my books. "I'm going to the student-teacher volleyball game," I tell him.

Henri looks less than thrilled with my announcement. "Did you discuss this with your mother?"

I stand tall, trying to look regal like Mam or Georgie can do without even trying. "How could I? I only just found out about it."

"Then I'll have to insist you come home with me."

"No. You all agreed I should go to school and get out of the house and have a normal routine. Well, this is part of the routine. I'll be home later. You tell Mam for me." I turn on my heel and walk beside Jasmine back toward the school, knowing that Henri is probably turning a hundred shades of red.

"You really told him!"

My hands are shaking. Yeah, I told him. And chances are, if Mam is feeling at all like herself, when I get home I'll likely be grounded for life. It probably isn't worth it just to watch a bunch of people I don't know play volleyball, but whatever. I'm tired of being told I can't do things. So I'm doing this.

In the gym, the bleachers have been pulled out, and people are crowding onto them, clumped together in friend groups. I follow Jasmine up to the top, where Marly and Jordan have saved us seats. On the way, we pass Bethany, Kim, and Miles, and I start to say hi, but Jasmine pulls me along, and Bethany turns away as if she doesn't see me.

Perhaps I am not such an underdog after all, if Bethany has turned on me. But is that good or bad?

Jasmine pulls out her phone and takes a selfie of the two of us. "Princess Power!" she says as she uploads it. "You need to make another video, in English, and let me be in it."

"I'm never sure what to say to Americans. My message has been for the people of my country."

"Let me do the talking then," Jasmine says.

"No," I say. "Not unless I know what you are going to say. This is too important to take chances."

Jasmine frowns, and I know I've annoyed her. "You don't trust me?"

I give her my best regal look. "I barely know you, and not that long ago you dumped a tray of food on my head. Let's say I'm being cautious."

Slowly, Jasmine's frown turns into a grin. "You're not so stupid, you know that?"

"I do," I answer, returning her grin.

"But I can be in the video, right?"

"Sure." I don't see a problem with that. I need a minute to think of a message—and one that is addressed to Americans.

A hundred conversations swirl around me, and I wonder if I will even be able to be heard in a video, but it's worth a try. I pull out my phone and position it so that Jasmine and I can both be seen. "*Hallo*, America! I am Princess Fredericka!"

"Fritzi!" Jasmine hisses in my ear. "It sounds friendlier."

Princess Fritzi? Well, why not.

"My friends call me Fritzi," I say. "I am about to watch a student-teacher volleyball game and am wishing that differences could be solved by a simple game in my country."

"Colsteinburg," Jasmine pipes up. "You have to tell them that part."

"*Ja*. Colsteinburg." This video is already almost too long. Time to wrap it up. I can't think of a snappy ending, so I finish with my traditional "*Prost!*"

"What's that mean?" Jasmine asks, camera still running.

"Cheers," I say.

"Then, cheers!" she says to the camera, and I stop filming. "Be sure to add the hashtag FeistyFritzi when you upload it. And maybe PrincessPower too."

I nod and do as she says. It can't hurt.

The teachers win the game handily. They win because they have more experience and are better organized and are stronger. If the two sides of the Colsteinburg coup were the teams, wouldn't our side win? Aren't we more experienced and better organized and stronger? But what if we're not? That's the thought that makes my stomach knot up.

"Too bad the students lost," I say as we descend the bleachers.

Bethany, whom I wasn't even talking to, is the one who answers.

"I suppose you think that if they had let the princess on the team they would have won, right? You think you're so great."

I'm so shocked I can barely think of a comeback, but this cannot go unanswered.

Jasmine springs to my defense. "She would have done a lot better than you. And you barely say boo to anyone. How come you're heaping on the princess? You on the side of the rebels or something?"

"I just don't like it when people put on airs," Bethany says, shrinking a bit under Jasmine's gaze.

"Well, when you see Fritzi putting on airs, you let us know. In the meantime, shut up."

Bethany turns away, and there isn't really anything for me to add, so I follow Jasmine off the bleachers and out of the gym.

"Thanks for that," I say when we get outside.

"Oh, you hardly need me standing up for you," Jasmine says. "I know you can hold your own. But she's so easy to fluster, I can't resist. Besides, she's being unfair to you."

She is being unfair to me, and I don't like it. I know it shouldn't matter, but somehow I have to convince Bethany that being a princess does not make me a bad person.

Outside, people are leaving for home or calling for rides. I half expect Henri to still be there waiting for me, but he's not. No one is.

"Do you have to call your bodyguard or anything to have him come get you?" Jasmine asks.

"I do," I say. "The only way I was allowed back at school was if Henri brought me back and forth. They are worried about security," I say.

"I guess that makes sense," Jasmine says.

I text Henri to let him know he can come get me.

"One more video while you wait," Jasmine says.

Why not?

"*Hallo!* Princess Fritzi here," I say, and Jasmine smiles approvingly. "With my friends Jasmine, Marly, and Jordan." I make sure they each get seen. "The teachers won. The sun is shining. It is lovely here in America, but my heart yearns for Colsteinburg. For home. *Prost!*"

"Cheers!" Jasmine adds.

I post the video. "Thanks for your help," I say.

"I hope it works," Jasmine says. "I'd like to be able to say I helped save a kingdom."

"You and me both," I answer. I look in the direction of the townhouse to see if Henri is in sight yet. Maybe I should walk toward there. That couldn't be any more dangerous than waiting here. I turn back toward the school to see if Jasmine wants to walk that way with me when I spot Felix coming up behind her.

Is he on our side or not? I can't be sure. I do know I don't want to deal with him on my own, or at all, if I can help it. He seems to have no such hesitancy about dealing with me. Before I can even formulate a plan, he's by my side.

"Your Royal Highness," he says, with all the proper deference I'm used to receiving when I'm home.

I nod my head in acknowledgment of the greeting but say nothing.

"I thought we had a deal," he says.

"I made the video," I say, taking a step back.

He takes a step closer, leaving the distance between us the same, and too close if you ask me. I can smell him. He smells like sweat and cologne and onions. It's not a good combination.

"And you deleted it."

"Ambassador Hart told me if the king leaves the kingdom, it's as good as abdicating."

His eyes narrow, and then he grins and makes a gesture with his hand as if to brush away that concern. "And you believe him?"

"Shouldn't I?" I ask. Of course I trust Ambassador Hart. He's letting us live in his house, after all. But what if that is a trap? How can we possibly know?

"You do know that he was quite tight with Francisco Orcutt when he was ambassador, don't you?"

"Was he?" I ask, my knees starting to take on the consistency of wet noodles. It's true his wife has been in touch with Mrs. Orcutt; she told us so. "But so were we all," I point out.

"Ah." Felix nods as if he understands. "It is difficult to know who to trust in a situation like this. But tell me, who brought you your teddy bear?"

"You did," I say.

"And who wants to help King Frederick get back on the throne?"

I don't know. God help me, I have no idea.

"You?" I say because it seems like the answer he wants.

"Of course, me. You need to convince Frederick to come here. Can you do that?"

"I don't know," I say. "I'm just a kid. No one listens to me."

"He'll listen," Felix says and takes hold of my arm.

Jasmine and her friends are still here, and now she is by my side brandishing her phone as if it were a weapon.

"Is this guy bothering you?" Jasmine asks.

"This is private business," Felix says.

"I want you to let go of me," I say and try to jerk my arm free from his grasp, but he's much stronger than I am.

"I'm not going to hurt you," he says.

"She says to let go," Jasmine says. "I've got 911 on speed dial.

Let go of her, or the police will be here so fast your head will spin."

He lets go of my arm. "I'll speak to you later, Your Royal Highness," he says and lopes off, not looking back at us. My heart is beating double-time.

"Who was that guy?" Jasmine asks, stepping close to me as if she might hold me up in case I start to fall.

"Some guy from back home."

"Whose side is he on?"

"I'm not sure," I answer. My breathing is starting to return to normal.

"We'll walk you toward your house and meet Henri. How's that sound? Besides, I kind of don't want to run into him again anyway. He creeps me out. Maybe I can have my mom pick us up at your place?"

"Let me just check with my sister to see if it's okay if you come over," I say.

"Not your mom?" Marly asks.

"My mam is having a little trouble with everything," I admit. I don't want to say anything against Mam, but it's the truth. "My sister has been taking care of things."

"My mom was like that when my dad left," Marly says, kicking a stone down the sidewalk. "Don't worry, it will get better."

It will get better, that's what I need to hear. I take a deep breath. Everything will be okay. "Yes," I say. "As soon as we're back with my pap, I'm sure it will be much better."

"Just give it time," Jasmine advises.

"It's hard," I admit.

"I know," Marly says. "But it'll be okay."

I really do have friends again. It feels good.

Regardless, I send a text to Georgie to let her know, to make sure Mam at least is not in her bathrobe or something. All I really want right now is to be safe behind locked doors.

"Ooh," Jordan says with a little skip. "We'll get to meet your sister and mother. I've never met a queen before. Do we have to bow or anything?"

"No bowing," I say. "That's only for the citizens of Colsteinburg. And ..."

"I know," Marly says, as if reading my mind. "Your mom might not be at her best. We get it."

Henri meets us before we get to the first traffic light. "You should have stayed where you were," he admonishes me.

"I couldn't," I say. "Felix was there."

Henri's eyebrows come together as his whole face transforms into a frown. "What did he want?"

"He says he really is Pap's friend. What do you think?"

"Until you encountered him the other day, I had no reason to doubt his allegiance to the royal family."

"So, you think he's on our side?"

"It is not for me to say," he says. Though truthfully, as head of security, saying who is and who is not on our side is kind of for him to say. We all get into his car, and he drives us to the condo.

Once we get there, Henri ushers us inside. He shuts the door behind us, and we are all safe. Georgie is sitting on the sofa. I don't see Mam. Maybe she's taking a nap. That might be for the best.

"Georgie, these are my friends." Is it too soon to call them friends? "Jasmine, Jordan, and Marly."

"Nice to meet you," Georgie says.

"Jasmine's mom is going to pick them up here. Felix was by the school, and he creeped us out," I explain.

Georgie frowns at the mention of Felix. "Very prudent," she says.

"Are you really going to be a queen some day?" Jordan asks.

"It's looking less and less likely," Georgie says with a hint of bitterness.

"Might as well sit down," I say to the girls. "Where's Mam?" I ask Georgie.

She lowers her voice before answering. "Upstairs. She wasn't up for company. Thanks for the warning."

"We're not going to get to meet the queen?" Jordan asks, disappointed.

"Not this time," Georgie says. She sits down, crossing her legs at the ankles, her hands folded primly in her lap, the model of the perfect princess. "Tell me, girls, what kinds of things should Fritzi get involved in around here? What is there to do?"

I lean against the doorjamb. "I thought we were moving."

"But we will probably stay local," Georgie says.

"Not much," Jordan says. "It's a lame neighborhood. Tell us what it's like where you really live. What do you do there?"

"We go to balls all the time," I say. "It's like living in a movie."

Georgie twists around in her chair so she can give me a withering look. "You've been to one ball, young lady. Why don't you tell your friends what they really want to know?"

They want to know that my life is like a movie, but it really isn't. Never has been. It would be easy to say that as the princesses, we can do whatever we want, but that isn't true. Being in the royal family actually means there are a lot of restrictions on us. We always have to be thinking of appearances. And then again, when we are at school, there are gobs of rules.

"I played netball," I answer.

"What's that?" Jasmine asks.

"Kind of like basketball," I say. She nods at this, as if things are starting to fit together in her mind.

"So, is there like a palace team or something?" Jordan asks.

I picture playing netball in the ballroom. The staff would have a conniption.

"I play it at school," I say.

"She goes to boarding school in France," Georgie explains.

"Don't you?" Marly asks.

"I graduated in June. But at school, there are lots of clubs and things to be involved in."

"Oh, we have clubs at our school," Marly says, seeming surprised that she found something in common with royalty.

"Most of the clubs are lame," Jasmine responds in a world-weary way.

"Well, yeah, that's true," Marly says. "But we do have them."

Jasmine looks at her phone and then out the window. "My mom is here." She stands up, and Marly and Jordan follow.

"Watch out for that guy," she says. "I don't trust him."

"Me either," I say. "I'll be careful."

They leave, and I lock the door behind them.

If only I knew whose side he was on. Life is so much easier if you know who to trust.

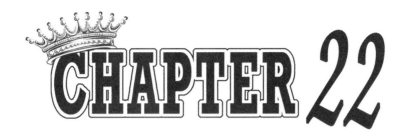

CHAPTER 22

I sit on the sofa and stick my hands under my legs to keep them from shaking. Everything is fine. There is no reason to panic. Everything is fine.

Everything is not fine.

"He said he was on our side and we couldn't trust the Ambassador," I say to Georgie. "And Henri thinks he's trustworthy. Or has been in the past. He wants me to do another video convincing Pap to come. What do I do? Which is the right thing?"

Georgie strides across the room and wraps her arms around me. "Don't do anything," she says. "Pap will know what he has to do without our interference. If there's anyone we know we can trust in all this, it's Pap."

She is right, of course. Pap doesn't need my opinion on what he should do, and he probably wouldn't follow it anyway. "But what if we can't trust the Harts?"

"They're letting us use their townhouse," Georgie reminds me.

"But what if it's a trick?"

Georgie hugs me a little tighter. "Grandma always said to trust your instinct with people, right?" she says, holding my hand in hers.

I nod. That was one of Grandma's many lessons to us.

"Yes, but my instinct is all confused these days. I thought we could trust Mr. Orcutt, and clearly we can't."

"Well, my gut says we trust the Harts," Georgie says. "They didn't have to help us, and they are. If they weren't on our side, why would they? What kind of trick could it be?"

"I don't know! I don't have the mind of a master villain! I don't know what someone might do."

Georgie's mouth turns up in a smile, and I can tell she's trying not to laugh at me.

"I suppose I should be glad you are not a master criminal in the making. I might be nervous sharing a bed with you."

She's trying to make me feel better, and it's working, even if just a bit. I smile too. "I guess that's one career path off the table."

"There are plenty of others," she says with a grin.

"So what do we do?" I ask.

"What we've been doing."

"It doesn't feel like enough," I say and sag into the sofa.

"Sometimes things take time," Georgie says. "It's only been

two weeks."

"Two weeks too long," I mutter.

Georgie sighs. "I agree with you, but try to be patient."

I'm twelve. I don't do patient.

"Come on, let's have a soda. That will make you feel better."

It can't hurt, I suppose. We go into the kitchen and are just popping open the cans when the doorbell rings.

"Maybe someone is bringing us pizza," Georgie says.

"Why would someone bring us pizza?" I ask.

"A girl can dream, can't she?"

I laugh. "Dream big, Georgie, dream big."

"What are you doing here?" we hear Henri ask, suspicion in his voice, to whoever is at the front door. So, probably not pizza. I peek out of the kitchen area toward the front door and see Felix on the threshold.

I grab Georgie's arm. "It's Felix. He's here! Why would he be here? Do you think Henri will let him in?"

"Hush!" Georgie urges as she peers past me to the front of the house. I notice she's not laughing anymore. "Henri won't let anything happen to us. He'll get rid of him."

But instead of slamming the door in his face, Henri is letting him inside.

"Georgie!" I hiss, digging my fingernails into her arm.

She disengages my hand from her arm. "Henri must be sure he's on our side," she says. "There's no other reason he'd let him in. Everything is going to be okay, Fritzi. Don't panic."

I don't know. Panic seems to be my default emotion right now.

Henri comes into the kitchen. "Georgie, go get your mother."

"Why is Felix here?" I ask. "Is he on our side?"

"He is," Henri says. "He has a message for your mother. Please go get her."

Even though only one of us has to give the message, I'm not leaving Georgie's side. I follow her like a shadow up the stairs.

Georgie knocks twice on Mam's door and then enters without waiting for a response. Mam is sitting on her bed, a book open on her lap. She looks at us expectantly.

"Mam," Georgie says. "That man, Felix Martel, is here. Henri let him in. He says he's on our side and that he has a message for you."

Mam puts her book aside, a look of relief on her face. "I didn't think Felix would really betray us. He's always been such a loyal adviser."

"But what about him wanting me to make the video so Pap would come here and then he'd lose the country? What about that?"

"Perhaps you misunderstood him," Mam says. "Felix knows as well as I do that under the circumstances, for Frederick to leave would be admitting defeat."

Maybe I did misunderstand him. It's been known to happen. He seemed pretty clear in what he wanted, but maybe I was wrong. I must have been wrong.

I like the sound of this. Felix is really on our side. He is here with a message for Mam. Maybe even a message from Pap. We need to go down and see what it is.

Downstairs, Felix greets us with a courteous bow of his head. “Your Majesty, it is so good to see you again. Your Royal Highnesses, you are both a vision, as always.”

The tone is right, the words are fine, but still a lingering ache sits in the pit of my stomach. He did bring me Sir Fred, and Sir Fred was not booby-trapped or bugged. I suppose I really should trust him.

“Shall we sit?” Mam suggests, and she leads me and Georgie to the sofa, where she sits between us. Felix sits in the armchair, and Henri stands like a sentinel by the door.

“I am here,” Felix begins, “because Frederick believes you are in danger.”

Mam stiffens and clutches my hand tighter.

“Have you spoken with him?”

“I have, and he wants you moved to a safe space. He is going to meet you there in a day or two.”

“Thomas Hart is looking for a safe space for us right now,” Mam says. “We know this place has been compromised by the media presence.”

“You cannot trust Thomas Hart. He’s the one who alerted the media. You need to go someplace unknown to him.”

Could it have been Mr. Hart who told the media where we were, and everyone was just blaming it on me and my videos? It’s possible. And even likely. So it’s Mr. Hart we can’t trust, and we can trust Felix. My head is swimming.

"And you have someplace for us to go?" Mam asks, one eyebrow arched.

"I do," he says, hands clasped casually around one knee.

"And Frederick is going to meet us there?"

"He is."

"Why has he not contacted us?"

"Like I said, your safety has been compromised, and he was afraid to contact you directly, being uncertain who might intercept his message."

"And he is coming here?" Mam asks. "But if he leaves, he abdicates. He knows that. Is he abdicating?"

"Not if no one knows he's left the country," Felix assures her, and he sounds so certain that I start to relax. He is one of Pap's advisers. He knows what's best for us. He is working for us. Things will work out. "And believe me," Felix says, "Frederick is very eager to be reunited with all of you again. He says once you are together, he promises you'll never be separated again."

This does not have the comforting effect Felix might have hoped it would.

"He said that?" I ask. "Those exact words? He said he promised?"

"Yes. That's what he said. He said he promised you. And you know your father would never break a promise to you."

What I know is that my father would never make a promise he can't fulfill. When we left and I asked him to promise me we'd be together soon, he said his word was enough and he would not make promises that might be impossible to keep. If he wouldn't make a promise to me then, when I was so scared, he certainly wouldn't send a message that he was promising us something.

Felix is lying.

I stand up. "Excuse me, I need a drink," I say, ignoring the fact that I am still holding my can of soda, and head to the kitchen.

Georgie follows me. "What's wrong?" she whispers. There are no doors between the downstairs rooms, so there's no real expectation of privacy.

There are several things wrong. The first is that I think I'm going to throw up or pass out or something. I sit on the chair and put my head between my knees. Georgie takes the soda from me and hands me a glass of water.

I sit up and take a sip.

"He's lying to us," I say.

"I know."

"Pap would never say he promised."

"I know."

"Do you think Mam knows?"

"I think so," Georgie says, but I don't like the note of uncertainty in her voice.

"What do we do?"

"We don't go anywhere with him, that's for sure," she says. "And we get him out of here. No harm done."

Georgie pokes her head through the doorway. "Mam, can you come here?" she calls. "Fritzi needs you."

It's as good an excuse as any.

Mam comes into the kitchen and rushes to me. "Are you ill?"

"Felix is lying to us," I whisper.

She nods. "I know. I'll ask him to leave, and then we'll see what Thomas Hart has in the way of other places for us to live." She puts one hand on my head and the other on Georgie's. Mam is back. "It will be fine, girls. Trust me."

How can she stay so calm? My hands are shaking. I'm hot and cold all at the same time. We let the enemy in. Henri let the enemy in. How can we even trust Henri again?

Mam turns to go back into the living room, and Georgie starts to follow, but Mam raises a finger and says, "Stay out here for the time being, girls."

I don't need to be told twice.

In the living room, Mam, sounding more like herself than she has done since the ball, says, "I think it is time you leave, Felix."

"But Your Majesty," he protests. "Frederick asked me to do this for him."

"No," she says, very simply. "I do not think he did. It is time for you to leave."

I'm sure he's going to argue or grab her or do something to paint himself suddenly as public enemy number one, and Henri tenses, ready to intercede as needed, but nothing happens except that Felix bows slightly, says "as you wish," and leaves.

My whole body goes limp in relaxation. He's gone. Nothing bad happened.

In the living room, Henri says, "I believe that was a rash

decision, Your Majesty."

"It was my decision, Henri. Do you question me?"

"I am in charge of your security. You need to trust me."

"And I do," Mam says, "but I did not trust him."

I don't know if Henri is going to answer that or not, because the front door smashes open, and Felix is back, flanked by two men with guns. Georgie and I duck under the kitchen table, for whatever protection that will give us.

Shots are fired, and I try to scream, but I don't think any sound comes out.

We need to call someone. Georgie has her phone in her hand. Whom do we call? I know no one's numbers. Not even Jasmine's.

Jasmine.

"Call 911," I whisper to Georgie. "Jasmine said that was the emergency number." At least I hope that's what she meant when she said she had 911 on speed dial.

Also, Jasmine watches my videos.

Maybe, just maybe, she could send help if I asked that way.

I pull the phone out of my back pocket, even as more shots and shouts are heard from the living room. Who is shooting? Has someone been hit? Is Mam okay?

I need to focus.

I turn on the camera.

"Fritzi here," I say in English. "Jasmine. Anyone. If you see this, send help. The police. Quick."

I upload it.

Next to me, Georgie is giving the person on the other end of her call the address.

One way or another, help has to come to us.

From the living room, Felix calls. "Fredericka, Georgiana, get in here. I want everyone where I can see them."

That means Felix is not dead. It means Felix is in charge. Oh, please, God, please let help come.

Georgie and I clasp hands. What will we find when we go into the living room?

Two men with guns stand by the front door.

Henri lies on the floor, bleeding, and Mam kneels over him trying to help. His eyes are open, and he is gasping for breath, but he's not dead. I only hope help comes in time.

Felix points a handgun at us.

"Sit," he says.

We sit.

I'm clutching Georgie's hand so tightly my fingers hurt.

"Cassandra," Felix says. "Go sit by your daughters."

"You need to get help for this man," Mam says, ignoring the utter rudeness of him calling her by her first name.

"You'll all need help if you do not do what I say," he responds.

Mam comes, and we move apart enough for her to sit between us. We both need to be sitting next to our mam right now. She takes our hands and holds on tight. At least we're alive.

For now.

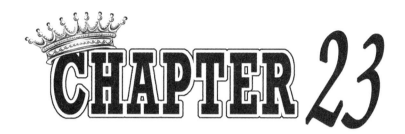

CHAPTER 23

The men with the guns stand near the door. The guns are not pointed at us, but I don't have any doubt that it would take less than a second for the men to have us in their sights. Felix paces in front of Henri.

"We could have done this the easy way," Felix says, "but one way or another, we'll get this done." He turns his attention to me. "Fredericka, you've been making videos."

It's not exactly a question, so I say nothing, just clutch Mam's hand tighter.

"We're going to make a video here. I need you to send a message to Frederick," he says. I notice he does not call him King Frederick, as would be right and proper. Is it already all over? Is there really no chance of getting back the kingdom?

"You will make a plea to your husband and father, telling him he should abdicate and let the country move on into the twenty-first century."

"But he shouldn't," I say.

The men with the guns shift their position slightly, and I cower back against Mam.

"He should," Felix says calmly. "I've written out what you each should say." He hands us each a sheet of paper. "Of course, you can always give him the message in your own words. That might be even more convincing."

My pre-written message is short and sweet. "I love you, Pappy, and want you to do what is best for your country and your family. Please abdicate now." I crumple up the paper. I will never tell my father to give up the crown. Never.

Felix holds his phone, which is apparently how he's going to film us.

Mam is composing herself. She doesn't look happy, but she does look like the queen. Georgie sits on the other side of Mam. All three of us like props on this sofa, ready to try to get my father to give up. It's disgraceful.

"I'm ready," Mam says.

"Good. You may start."

My shoulders tense. My stomach aches. Tears come to my eyes. There is a lump in my throat so large I'm sure I'll never be able to speak over it.

Mam sits up straighter and begins. "I am Cassandra Sophia

Maria von Boden don Mohr. This is a message for my husband, Frederick. The girls and I are safe and well, for now." Her paper is folded in her lap. I don't know what it says or if she's sticking to the script or not. "It is important that you let it be known that you abdicate the throne of your fathers and grandfathers. It is time for Colsteinburg to move forward. Without us." She stops speaking. I don't know if they expected her to say more or not, but she's clearly done.

I clench my jaw. I will not ask my father to abdicate. I will not.

Georgie starts speaking next. She's not reading from her paper either. "I am Georgiana Sophia Francesca von Boden don Mohr, the heir apparent to the throne of Colsteinburg. If my father, Frederick, king of Colsteinburg, abdicates, I will renounce my claim to the throne."

She stops short of telling him to abdicate, but what is she doing? Renouncing her future claim? No! She can't do that. It's not right! Does that make me next in line after Pap? It would. If she renounces her claim, then I'll be next in line to the throne. Well. I'm not renouncing anything.

It's my turn.

"I am Princess Fredericka Elisabetta Teresa von Boden don Mohr. Don't do it, Pap! Don't give up. Why should we give up our country?" I have more to say, but the swift and hard slap across my face silences me.

I taste blood in my mouth from where my braces bit into my cheek.

Mam jumps up. “Don’t you hit her. She’s just a little girl.”

“She’s a nuisance,” Felix says.

I don’t mind at all if this rebel thinks I’m a nuisance. I’d smile except my mouth hurts too much.

Felix points to one of the men with the guns. “Take her away.”

What? Are they going to execute me right here and now? Well, I’m not going down without a fight. Felix still holds his phone. I’m not sure if he’s still filming or not.

“If you are going to kill me, you might as well just do it right now, right here,” I say.

Mam jumps in front of me, shielding me from any possible harm.

“You will not touch this child,” she says.

“Then that child better shut up,” Felix hisses.

Georgie leans close to me. “Please, Fritzi, don’t make things worse.”

Things can’t get any worse.

Or maybe they can. Right now he hasn’t actually killed us, but I suppose, what with him having armed guards and all, that the possibility is on the table.

Felix turns the camera to himself. “Frederick. Understand this. Your family is under our control. You have twenty-four hours to make your decision. Your kingdom or the life of your family. We’ll start the executions with the one who did not renounce her claim to the throne.”

My knees go weak, and my fingers are pure ice. I think I’m

going to be sick.

Mam grabs me in a hard hug. "They will not hurt you, darling, I promise."

"Not if we get what we want," Felix says, and he pockets his phone. I don't know where he'll upload the video. It's too long for lots of sites, but maybe he'll put it on the web, or maybe he really does know where Pap is and will simply send it to him without making it public.

I curl up in a corner of the couch, my legs no longer able to hold me up. The men with guns guard the front and back doors.

"Why couldn't you simply cooperate?" Mam asks me, but her voice is gentle, and she rubs my back in a soothing gesture.

"Because I'm a princess, and I want to stay a princess," I say, muttering the words into my knees.

Georgie sits next to me and puts her arm around me. "So am I, Fritzi, but it's not all that we are."

"What else are we?" I ask. All my life, I've been told to do or not do certain things because I was a princess. It is who I am; it is coded in my DNA. I can't stop being one.

"We are a family," Georgie says. "You are my little sister. You are smart and funny and brave and can do any number of wonderful things if you set your mind to it. But they don't have to involve a royal title."

I don't believe her.

"What are you going to do if you're not the next queen of Colsteinburg?" I ask, sniffling.

"I'm not sure," she says. "There's a world of possibilities out there."

I can't be as optimistic as Georgie. I can't see past tomorrow, when apparently I'll be the first one killed. I uncurl myself and wipe my nose.

"Phones on the table," Felix says. "I know you each have one."

Georgie and I take our phones from our pockets and put them on the table.

"Cassandra?" Felix says. I want to punch him each time he calls her by her first name.

"Mine is upstairs. We need to call for help for Henri."

Felix looks at Henri. His eyes are closed now, but his chest still rises and falls regularly. He's not dead. "I didn't hit anything too vital, it can wait," he says.

But how long?

Oh, please let help come. Shouldn't the police be here by now?

"Hans, escort Cassandra to retrieve her phone."

"I do not need an escort," Mam says and heads up the stairs.

"I think you do," Felix calls after her, and Hans follows Mam, leaving the front door unguarded. Felix is so sure that we are under his control that he isn't even looking at the door but upstairs after Mam. Moving slowly at first, I edge closer to the door, and when I'm within a few feet, I rush to it. I'm turning the knob when Felix grabs me around my waist, lifting me off the ground.

"Not smart, little one. Not smart at all."

He's squeezing me hard, and I'm having trouble breathing.

Mam comes back down, phone in hand. "Put her down!" she demands.

"She tried to get away."

"And would you have any respect for any of us if we didn't?" Mam asks, and I want to cheer. The queen has found her voice again.

Felix drops me to the ground, pushing me toward the sofa. Mam rushes toward me.

"Cassandra! Put that phone on the table."

She does but gives Felix such a look of disdain that I'm surprised he doesn't wither away.

The other guard has been searching for landline phones and disabling them, removing batteries or cords as the case may be. He's taking no chances.

"We need to get help for Henri," Mam says once again.

Felix glances at Henri's still form and shrugs, but a look of uncertainty passes over his face.

"He's your friend," Mam implores. "Or at least he was. You can't just let him die."

With a resigned sigh, Felix says, "Fine, you and Georgiana can tend to him, Cassandra."

"He needs competent medical help," Mam protests.

Another shrug. "I think you're his best bet right now."

"Too bad I wasn't a nurse during the war," Mam mutters.

"What war?" I ask.

"Any war," she answers. "You girls go upstairs and see what

kind of first aid supplies we have."

"They stay where they are," Felix says.

"Not if I need their help to keep this man alive." Mam has fire in her voice.

"Fine, they may go," Felix says and indicates with a wave of his hand that we may head upstairs. I think he just wants to feel like he's in command of things, which, really, he is. Who are we kidding?

Georgie and I find gauze pads and surgical tape, and other than some first aid cream and a bottle of Advil, that's about all there is. We bring these things downstairs to Mam, who looks at them with dismay. "That's it?"

I can see that the blood is coming from close to his shoulder on the left-hand side. That's near the heart, right? Does that mean there's no hope? But his eyes are open again, so that must be a good sign.

"Go bring me some water and soap and a washcloth," Mam instructs. "I'll do the best I can."

She cleans him up, applies pressure to the wound, bandages it, and gets the two thugs to carry Henri to the sofa, where he may be at least a little more comfortable.

Mam goes upstairs to clean up, and we follow her.

"Will Henri be okay?" I ask as Mam washes her hands.

"If we can get him to a doctor, he stands a chance. Otherwise, I don't know. I just don't know." She looks tired and frustrated, but also regal and angry. "I wish we had some good way of getting in touch with Frederick."

"Do you think he'll really abdicate?" I ask.

Mam turns on me.

"Do you think for one minute your father would rather hold on to the throne instead of you? If he hasn't already decided this is a lost cause, he'll not hesitate a second when he hears of the threat to you. Oh yes, he'll abdicate."

"I don't want him to," I say.

Georgie looks at me with a puzzled expression. "But they will kill you, maybe all of us, if he doesn't. Is that what you want?"

"No. But I don't want him to stop being king."

Mam's eyes look sad when she answers me.

"It may not be about what we want. Remember, a king who is king against the will of his people is a tyrant. Your father is not a tyrant."

He is no tyrant, it's true. Do I want him to stay king if that means him being considered a tyrant? I guess not. But he wouldn't be a tyrant if most people wanted him. How do we know that most people don't?

"Where is he?" Mam murmurs. "Is he even safe?"

The pain in my stomach threatens to overtake my whole being.

In the distance, the sound of sirens pierces the air.

My heart beats faster. Could it be? Are they coming here? They get louder and louder. They must be coming here. There is hope after all.

CHAPTER 24

The sirens are closing in. We will be rescued! I'm going to make sure Pap knights Jasmine, or whatever he can do to reward her for this, because either by seeing the video and calling the police or by giving me the clue for the emergency number, she has been instrumental to our rescue.

"Get down here!" Felix barks up the stairs. We don't move right away; after all, help is at hand. "Now!" Felix shouts, and then he is stomping up the stairs himself. "Didn't you hear me? I need you all downstairs. Now!"

Since we still don't move fast enough for him, he grabs me around the waist and lifts me off the floor again. Being the smallest really stinks sometimes. At first I'm not even scared, and then I feel the cold steel of the gun barrel touch my temple.

"Mam," I whimper.

"Put her down!" Mam demands.

"I will not. She's my insurance policy. Now, all of you. Downstairs."

This time, Mam and Georgie head down the stairs, and Felix follows, still carrying me. I would struggle to get away, but the gun to my head scares me into submission. I'm letting myself be carted around like a ragdoll, and I don't like it, but I don't know how to do anything about it.

The sirens are now right outside. The men with the guns break the front window and start shooting before the police car even stops. Felix moves the gun from my head long enough to open the front door.

"Where are you taking her?" Georgie screams and grabs at my arm.

"Behave, and no one gets hurt," he growls.

Georgie holds me for a second longer, and I feel something being shoved in my back pocket. My phone? Hopefully.

Now the door is open, and I see the police officer hunkered down behind his car, gun pointed at the townhouse. There is only one police car, and the officer is on the radio, obviously calling for reinforcements. One police officer is not going to be able to help at all in this situation.

"Call for an ambulance!" I scream to the officer, hoping he hears me. "Someone's been shot."

"Be quiet, Princess," Felix hisses.

He carries me out of the house to a car and shoves me inside. The police officer, still taking cover from the gunfire, can do nothing to help.

"Where are we going?" I ask as Felix steps on the gas and drives away, with me as a captive in his car.

"To a nice safe place where you can wait for your father to come for you."

"He won't come for me. He's busy saving the kingdom."

"He'll save you instead."

Part of me wants that to be true, and part of me doesn't. The best I can do is make sure that he can't use me as a pawn. I need to get away.

Soon he has to stop at a traffic light, and I'm sure the only reason he doesn't run it is because the car in front of him is stopped. It's not much of a chance, but it's the only one I've got. I hit the unlock button, open the door and jump out of the car, running back the way I came and ducking down the first side street I come to.

I know he's going to follow me, but if I can get some distance between us, I might be able to lose him. I run blindly up and down streets, ducking into alleys between buildings and hoping beyond hope that I don't run into a dead end at some point.

I come out of one alley onto what looks like a fairly main street. There are restaurants and stores and lots of people. I stop and catch my breath and look behind me. I don't see Felix anywhere, so I take that as a good sign. I don't know where I am. I'm not near the school. I'm not even sure which direction the townhouse is in from here. I stand on the sidewalk, nearly paralyzed with indecision. Where should I go? Even if I knew how to get to the townhouse, that probably wouldn't be the safest place to head. I need to be someplace safe so Felix can't get me, otherwise I'll always be on the run.

What I should do first is let Pap know I'm okay. If he sees the video Felix made, he'll think he needs to come here to rescue me, but I don't need rescuing. He needs to stay with the kingdom.

I reach around to my back pocket. My phone is there. Yay for Georgie keeping her head when all around her people were losing theirs. I duck into the doorway of a vacuum repair store and start taping.

"Prinzessin Fredericka here," I begin. "Pap, I am safe. Do not fear for me. Stay with the country, and save the kingdom. Remember you are king. *Ich leibe dich.*"

I hope that is enough. I shove my phone back into my pocket and move quickly down the street, turning down the first side street I come to. I need to keep moving so that Felix can't find me. And I need to get help. I need to find a policeman. There should be one on nearly every corner directing traffic, right? I've watched American movies. I know how this works, but I haven't seen one yet. I pull my phone back out of my pocket as I walk and dial 911, remembering that I don't have to find the police. They can send them to me.

On the other end of the phone, a pleasant female voice says,

"911, what is your emergency?"

"I need a policeman," I say.

"What is the emergency?" the woman repeats. "Why do you need a policeman?"

"Someone was trying to kidnap me, and I got away, but I don't know where he is, and I need a policeman." I keep walking as I talk, and the simple act of telling what is wrong makes me panicky. This is real, this is really happening.

"Okay, where are you?" the woman says, her voice steady and calm.

I take a breath. I can do this. I can stay calm as well. "I don't know. Somewhere near Boston."

"Are you inside or outside?"

"Outside."

"What street are you on?"

"I don't know," I say, looking for a cross street and a street sign.

"Can you find out?"

"I'll try."

"What phone number are you calling from, in case we get disconnected?"

I tell her, but it's a foreign number and that confuses her.

"What is your name?" she asks.

"I am Fredericka Mohr." I answer. "Please can you send the police? I'm afraid."

"You need to tell us where you are," she says. "Did you find a street name?"

I see a cross street and hurry to it. I tell her the names on the sign.

"Okay, you stay there, and we'll have a police officer with you shortly."

"I can't stay here. If I stay in one place, he'll find me."

"But we need to find you, Fredericka. Just stay calm. Someone will be with you soon."

I scan the street and see what looks like the car that Felix forced me into before.

"I see him," I try to scream, but it ends up as more of a whisper. "He's back. I need to get out of here."

"Fredericka," the woman begins, but I'm not listening. I need to get out of here. I shove the phone back in my pocket and run down the side street, hoping Felix didn't see me before I saw him. I turn down one street and then another, hoping that by not keeping a straight line, Felix won't be able to follow me.

Then as I turn down a street that is more residential, with cookie-cutter houses lining both sides, I see Bethany, walking with Kim and coming toward me. They will help me. I'm saved.

"Boy, am I happy to see you!" I say, finally stopping to catch my breath.

"Hello, Fritzi," Kim says and nudges Bethany, who looks like she's searching for an escape route. I know the feeling.

"What are you doing here?" Bethany asks. "I thought you were trapped at home waiting for the police. I guess that was just a pathetic attempt at getting a little more attention. Saying you were a princess didn't get you enough?"

I'm not even sure what she's talking about, but I can't waste time trying to figure it out. "Do you know where the police station is?" I ask. "Or even a policeman? I've looked on the corners but didn't see one."

"This isn't the nineteen-fifties," Bethany says with a roll of her eyes. "Do you think America is like you see in old movies?"

"Of course I thought that," I answer, not in the mood to play games. "Why wouldn't I?"

"Just make another video," Bethany says. "Or didn't that one bring the police?"

"It did," I say and realize that she has admitted to watching my videos, but I don't have time to sort out what that actually means. "But I need a police officer. Now. I'm in danger."

"Call 911," Kim says.

"I did. But they didn't get here fast enough."

"She's probably so used to traveling with private security she's afraid to walk around without an armed guard," Bethany sneers as an aside to Kim, treating me like I'm not even there.

While that is scarily accurate in its own way, it falls a little short of reality.

"I just need the police," I say. I don't care if she's dissing me. This is no time to worry about injured pride. I need help, and they can help me. I know they can. "Please! Do you know where I can find them?"

Bethany shrugs as if it's no concern of hers. Kim screws up

her face in concentration. "I think the station is at the end of Main Street. You go right when you get to the corner and then just go straight."

I start to thank her when I'm distracted by a car pulling up behind them. My heart starts to beat faster even before Felix jumps out of the car. I don't wait for further explanations. I turn and start to run.

"Fredericka!" he yells after me. I glance behind and see that he's grabbed Bethany. I stop.

Her eyes are wide with fright. Kim runs away, hopefully to get help.

"Come here, Fredericka," he says.

Like a pull toy on a string, I go.

"You don't want to see anything happen to your friend, do you?" he asks.

"Let her go," I say, trying to sound regal and commanding like Mam. My voice comes out in a pathetic squeak instead.

"I will let her go as soon as you agree to come with me."

If I go with him, he will have power over me again. He will use me as bait to get Pap to abdicate. The whole future of the kingdom will be in jeopardy. Not to mention my life, since he's threatened to kill me tomorrow if Pap doesn't abdicate. If I go with him, there is no good outcome for me at all. None.

But if I don't go, what will he do to Bethany? She has nothing to do with any of this. She does not deserve to be caught in the middle of it. She might not like me because I'm not the underdog—

though in this particular situation I don't think I could get more underdog-ish—but no matter what I do, I lose.

I lose, yes. But not Bethany. A princess does not let others suffer on her behalf. That was another lesson taught by my grandmother.

"I'll go with you," I say. "Let her go."

He drops Bethany, shoving her away from him, and grabs me. I don't struggle. What's the point? If I escape here, he'll just grab Bethany again. He shoves me in the car and takes off again.

"Are you going to kill me?" I ask. He's got to know I'm thinking it; we might as well just get it out there.

"My, you are direct." He pretends to think about it for a moment. "If you prove to be no longer useful to me, then yes, probably." He grins at me; it is not a friendly grin. "I can be direct, too."

"Well, I don't think I'm going to be particularly useful to you, so you might as well kill me now," I say with a resigned sigh. I will not be a pawn to deceive my family or my country. Instead I will go down in the history books like the Romanov Sisters, as someone who died in a revolution.

I'd rather not, but if that's the way things have to be, I can be brave. Hopefully. For as long as it takes.

"Feisty Fritzi indeed," he says with a chuckle.

I don't think my imminent death is a topic for amusement.

"No, I think you can be useful to us," he says.

"I don't want to be useful to you," I say.

"I've gotten that impression."

We ride in silence for awhile. I don't know where we are going. We seem to be getting farther and farther from town and anything remotely familiar.

I don't want to die for the nobler cause. Perhaps I was too hasty when I said I wouldn't work with him. Maybe I can be forgiven for trying to save myself. It's not unreasonable to want to live until I can at least say I'm officially a teenager.

"There's no reason to be concerned," Felix says after probably a half hour of silence. "No one really wants to see you hurt. You have nothing to fear."

I don't feel particularly comforted by that.

We come to another town, and Felix pulls the car into an underground parking garage. Is this the end? In the movies, nothing good ever happens in a parking garage. If he is going to kill me, I hope it can be outside so my last view can be of something beautiful.

Felix pulls me from the car and drags me toward an elevator.

So maybe I won't die in the garage.

My blood starts to warm a little. Maybe I won't die at all.

Because, really, I'd rather not.

He drags me up a very industrial staircase to a slightly less industrial hallway. We seem to be in an office building, but no one is around. Maybe it's a closed office building. I'm not sure this is much better than a parking garage, to be honest.

He opens a door marked Suite 103, and we go in. There's a

standard-issue waiting room with semi-comfortable looking chairs and side tables with magazines on them. We don't stop in the waiting room though. He unlocks a door to the left and opens it. My whole body is shaking, and I don't know what to expect next, but something tells me it's not going to be good.

He reaches into my back pocket and extracts my phone. "You won't be needing this," he says and shoves me into the room.

Behind me, the door locks, and I find myself alone in an empty, windowless room.

Now what?

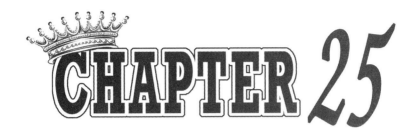

CHAPTER 25

At least the room has light. It's bad enough to be alone in an empty room, but to be alone in an empty room in the dark would be more than I could handle right about now.

I listen at the door but hear nothing on the other side. I go to the farthest corner of the room, somehow feeling that it's the safest, and sit down on the floor, my back against the wall. I wish I had my phone. Besides calling for help, I'd call Mam and let her know I'm alive. And I'd make another video. And what would I say? I picture it in my head.

"Princess Fritzi here. I've got myself in a bit of a muddle. I don't know where I am, and I am being used for bait so my father, the king, will abdicate. If anyone can figure out how to help me, well, I'd really appreciate it. *Danke.* Thanks."

Yeah. That would be helpful.

I could cry. It's very tempting to cry. But I realize I'm not as much sad as I am angry. How dare Felix kidnap me and use me to win the kingdom for Orcutt? That's not playing fair. Though maybe fairness doesn't have a whole lot to do with it right now.

My stomach grumbles, and I wonder if Felix will even bother to feed me. Maybe he'll just leave me in here all alone until I starve to death. He could have at least put a chair in the room. There are doors, and while I'm fairly certain they are not an escape route, I investigate. One is to a coat closet, empty except for one wire hanger. Maybe I can use that hanger to pick the lock on the door. I'll come back to that later.

The other room is a bathroom. As soon as I see the toilet, I realize that I really need to pee. Power of suggestion, possibly, but regardless, I'm really glad the facility is there. I wash my hands and cup them to get a little water to drink from the sink and then head back to see what I can do with the hanger.

I'm halfway across the room when the door opens, and Felix comes in carrying a bag of take-out food. "Hungry, Your Royal Highness?" he asks. I don't particularly like the sarcastic note in his voice, but I'm not in much of a position to do anything about it.

"Yes, thank you," I say, reaching for the bag.

"Not so fast," he says, holding it out of reach. "I think you'll have to work for your supper."

I'm pretty sure he doesn't mean hard labor in the copper mines.

"What do you want me to do?"

"I think you owe me another of your videos."

"I can't make a video. You took my phone," I remind him.

"I'll provide the phone," he says. "It's time to let the people of Colsteinburg know that they are no longer indebted in any way to the royal family."

I swallow hard, but I can't let his misunderstanding stand. "The people of Colsteinburg are not indebted to us and never have been," I say. "The royal family serves the people. We are there on behalf of the people."

The slap across the face surprises me just as much as last time. "None of this royalist hogwash," he says. "Make the video."

I hold my hand to my cheek and try not to let him see me cry.

"I don't think so," I say.

"Then I don't think you'll be eating." He leaves and takes the bag of food with him. The smell of burgers and fries lingers in the room, and I let the scent wash over me and pretend I'm eating. It's not very satisfying.

I grab the coat hanger that will free me from this prison and then study the lock. It's electronic. I don't think there is anything I can do with the coat hanger to open it, even if I had any idea how to pick a lock. My education up to this point has been sorely lacking in some crucial skills.

Back to my cozy corner. My stomach rumbles again. Maybe I should have done a video for him so I could get some food. But no. He already said he'd kill me tomorrow if Pap doesn't do what he wants. I'm not likely to starve to death before tomorrow, and I can at least go out without acting the traitor.

What happened at the townhouse after Felix took me? Who won, the police or the bad guys? Are Mam and Georgie okay? Did Henri get to a hospital? I pull my knees close to my chest and rest my head on them. I will not cry. I will not.

The doorknob rattles, and I look up.

Felix is there once again carrying the bag of food.

"One little video and you can have this burger," he says enticingly.

"No," I answer. I really want to say yes. I really want that burger, even if it's cold now.

"All you have to do is beg Pappy to come and save you. That's all I need."

"I won't do it!" I put my head back down on my knees. I don't want to look at him. I want this nightmare to be over.

"Fine. My way will be more effective anyway."

That doesn't sound good. Next thing I know, he's pulling me to my feet. He grabs hold of me from behind and holds a knife to my neck. With his other hand, he holds out his phone.

"Smile for the camera, Fritzi," he says.

I'm afraid to even move.

"Frederick. I have your daughter. She is entirely under my control. You have until noon tomorrow to let me know your answer, or she dies."

"Hey!" I protest as he lowers the camera. "You said he had

twenty-four hours. Noon isn't twenty-four hours!"

"I changed my mind. I'm in charge. I can do that."

He lets go of me, and I retreat back into my safe corner. I want to stand up to him and let him know who he's dealing with, but I'm tired and hungry and scared, and I just can't anymore.

"Can I have a blanket?" I ask, hating myself for even asking for that.

He hesitates, and I think he's going to say no, but finally he says, "I'll see if I can find one."

"Thank you," I answer, wishing I'd had the courage not to say anything at all.

He leaves the bag of food on the floor, but I don't touch it. I didn't do the video willingly. I didn't earn that food. It seems like forever before he comes back with a blanket and drops it by my feet. He picks up the bag in the middle of the floor. "You didn't eat your dinner," he says. "No sense in letting the food go to waste." He puts that by my feet as well.

He leaves again. I reach out for the bag of food. There's really no reason to deny myself the burger and fries, undoubtedly cold by this point, just because he made doing the video a condition of eating them. I can set my own conditions. And I say I'm hungry and I should eat the food that is available to me. So I do.

It's cold and kind of greasy, and it leaves my stomach feeling a bit unsettled, but it satisfies my hunger and it gives me something to do for a little while. There are only so many ways to occupy yourself in an empty room, while waiting to either die or be rescued.

I curl up with my blanket in my corner and say every prayer I can ever remember learning and make up a bunch of new ones. When you're waiting to die, praying seems like a really good way to pass the time.

I wake up when the door to the room opens again. I have no way of knowing how long I've slept. Was it an hour or ten? I'm stiff and achy, but I'm not used to sleeping on the floor for any amount of time, so that might not mean much.

Bleary-eyed, I watch Felix cross the room to me. "I hope you slept well," he says. I doubt he really cares, so I don't answer him.

"I have heard from your father. He is on his way to rescue his little princess. Only you won't be a princess anymore, will you?" He laughs at his own stupid attempt at a joke and leaves the room again.

Pap is coming here? I won't die. My heart soars at that, which feels like a betrayal. By rescuing me, he is abandoning the kingdom. I didn't want him to do that. Colsteinburg has been ours for eight hundred years. It should go on just the same for another eight hundred.

If I had my phone, I would check and see what time it is. I don't even have a window to see if it's morning or not. If I had my phone, I'd make another video, one last video as a princess.

"Prinzessin Fredericka here. Once upon a time, I was told I was a princess, and it was true. After today, it may not be true anymore, but my love for my country will never die. I want to come back and see the mountains and the flowers and the rivers.

Ich leibe dich, Colsteinburg."

The world as I know it is ending, regardless of what happens today. I don't even know how to look ahead beyond the next few hours. I don't know what life is going to look like. If I'm even going to be alive. I hug my knees to myself and try not to think about anything at all. It's hard.

Time drags on, and I don't know if it is a good thing or not that I can't check my phone every few minutes to see how slowly the time is passing.

The door opens one more time, and Felix stands there. "Come with me, Fredericka."

He didn't call me Princess. Is it already all over?

"Where am I going?" I ask, though why I should be at all reluctant to leave this empty room is beyond me. Maybe it's that I don't want whatever might happen next to happen.

"Time to see Pappy." He takes me by the arm and leads me out of the empty room to the one next door. This one is furnished with a sofa and a table, and standing in the middle of it is Pap.

"Fritzi!"

He is upon me in an instant, hugging me and kissing me.

I bury my face in Pap's shirt, inhaling the scent of him, sweat and cologne and a hint of tobacco, memorizing all of him in case we are separated again. I don't care what happens next. I'm with Pap, and that's all that matters.

"My precious Fritzi!" he keeps repeating as he strokes my hair.

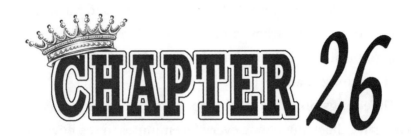

CHAPTER 26

"Very touching reunion," Felix says, his voice hard. "But there's really no time for that." He grabs me by the arm and separates me from Pap. I don't want to let go of him, and I can tell Pap feels the same way, but then I feel cold metal touching my forehead again. It only takes a second to realize it's a gun. The way Pap backs off, looking horrified, confirms that.

This has happened one too many times. I'm with Pap now, I'm supposed to be safe. I think I'm going to throw up.

"Now, Frederick," Felix says, his voice the epitome of reason and compromise. "There is a little matter of a paper that needs to be signed. Why don't you go do that now? That is if you don't want anything to happen to your little princess."

"What paper?" I manage to ask. I'm not sure how my voice

sounds so calm and steady. I don't feel calm and steady.

"Abdication papers. Your pappy signs them, and we can move on to having an elected government like all modern nations."

So, just being out of the country doesn't mean he's automatically abdicated. There is still a chance. Pap is moving toward the table, his shoulders hunched. He looks defeated. He wouldn't do this, he'd fight it, if he wasn't worried about me. I don't want to be the reason the monarchy is ousted after eight hundred years.

I have to fight back.

Out of the corner of my eye, I see a phone in Felix's shirt pocket. Is it mine? Without giving myself time to think about it, I grab the phone out of his pocket and start filming before Felix has a chance to realize what I'm doing.

"If the king abdicates, it is because there is a gun at my head." No time for anything more. Felix is already reaching for my phone, but with a speed that comes from practice, I upload the video. He grabs the phone from me, throws it on the floor, and stomps on it.

I flinch, and the gun barrel pushes into my temple. I really hope the video finished uploading before he did that.

"That was not very wise," he says.

I don't know. Seemed like my best option under the circumstances.

"Now everyone will know that it's not a real abdication. Even if you kill me, it won't count."

"Oh, it will count!" Felix growls.

"I'll sign," Pap says. "Leave her alone."

"You sign, and we'll discuss."

"Don't sign!" I say.

Pap looks at me. His eyes have a haunted look I don't ever remember seeing there before. "Fritzi, you matter more to me than being king, don't you know that?"

"Let your pappy sign the paper," Felix says, pushing the gun harder against my head.

There's a gun at my head.

He's going to kill me.

Any second now.

I throw up all over the floor.

Felix jumps back, away from me, moving the gun. Pap rushes toward me, taking me in his arms. "Oh, my poor girl."

He looks up at Felix. "Can you bring her a glass of water or something?"

He doesn't look like he's going to, but he takes in my smashed phone and the mess on the floor, and I suppose he figures we don't pose much of a threat, so he leaves the room, locking the door behind him as he goes.

Pap holds me, carries me to the sofa, and rocks me, soothing me. "Oh, my feisty Fritzi. 'Though she be but little, she is fierce.'" He smoothes my hair.

I let him hold me. I cry in big gulping sobs. I can't believe I threw up on the floor. It's so disgusting.

"We have to get out of here," I say.

"Hang tight," Pap says. "Let Felix bring you the water."

"He won't," I say.

"He will," Pap asserts.

"We need to check if the phone still works. We can call 911 for help."

Pap checks the phone, but it's no use. It's beyond repair.

Felix brings me a glass of water, and someone else comes in with a mop to clean up the floor, and then they leave us alone again.

Pap and I stay on the sofa, his arms wrapped securely around me. I feel safe like this, but a part of my brain acknowledges that I'm not really safe. Not yet.

"Has he hurt you at all?" Pap asks.

"No. Just tried to scare me."

"He certainly scared me," Pap says, "with the videos he sent of you."

"The one where Mam said to abdicate? She didn't mean it. We were forced. They had guns. We don't want you to abdicate."

He gives me an extra squeeze. "I know. You were very brave, but you don't have to protect me, sweetie. It's my job to protect you."

"I don't want you to stop being king," I say, sniffling into his shirt.

"You know, you will always be my princess, whether I'm king or not."

"It's not about being a princess." Though, honestly, part of it is. I like being a princess. "It's that Colsteinburg is our family's heritage. It's our country, handed down from generation to generation to guard and take care of. We can't just give that up. Not without a fight, at least."

"I'm afraid I'm not a very good king."

"You haven't had a lot of practice," I say. I've given this a bit of thought. "You weren't expecting to have to take over so soon. But you can do it. You know what King Franz and King George did. You know how. And we'll help."

Pap kisses the top of my head.

"Yes, I suppose we do have something worth fighting for," he says.

We sit in silence for a minute, just enjoying being near each other again.

"Are we going to fight back?" I ask.

"I don't want to risk anything happening to you, Fritzi," Pap says.

I appreciate that sentiment. "Then what are we going to do?"

"We'll try negotiating."

I suppose it was the only option other than completely giving in. We can't fight back, not against guns.

The door opens, and Felix walks in. "Is she feeling better?"

"Yes, thank you," Pap answers.

"Good. Now, let's get down to business. It's time you signed that paper."

"If I sign, it will be under duress."

"I don't really care, as long as you sign it."

"And what do I get out of it, if I sign?" Pap asks, starting to sound more like a king.

"Your little family gets to stay alive."

He nods. "And?"

"Isn't that enough?"

"Not really."

Felix frowns, looking frustrated. "What more do you want?"

"I would want a guarantee of continued safety for myself and my family."

Felix shrugs. "Eh, that is not up to me."

Pap gives me one more squeeze, and then he stands up. He is taller than Felix by several inches, and more muscular, and in general, much better looking—though I may be a bit biased.

"I will not give in to blackmail," Pap says, sounding strong and confident. I want to cheer for him.

"Sure you will," Felix says, his voice smooth and slimy.

The door opens once more, and this time, there are uniformed men with guns. Pap grabs me to him, but it is Felix who looks afraid this time, and with good reason: the guns are aimed at him.

"King Frederick, I assume," one of the armed men says.

"Yes," Pap says with surprising calmness.

"There's a car outside that will take you and your daughter to safety."

Pap takes me by the hand, and we walk past everyone. Outside, we find a black car with a driver waiting for us.

"King Frederick?" the uniformed driver asks.

"Yes," Pap says. We climb into the back of the car and find Ambassador Hart waiting for us.

"I finally got State Department protection for you," he says with a wink to me.

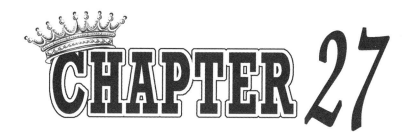

CHAPTER 27

The car brings us to an imposing building in the middle of Boston. Pap steps out of the car first and holds out a hand for me. I get out of the car, and he takes my arm as if I were as old as Georgie. Surrounded by security, we enter the marble and glass lobby. We barely pause before being put in an elevator and going to the top floor. There, the same security guards usher us into a reception room, where Georgie and Mam wait for us.

Mam hugs me so tight I think she's never going to let go, but then she does and she's in Pap's arms, and seeing the two of them together makes me so happy that tears come to my eyes. They should never be apart again. They are like two halves of a whole; when they are apart, they are just not themselves.

Georgie puts her arms around me and hugs me tight. "I was

so worried about you," she says.

"What happened?" I ask. "How did you get away from Hans and the other guy? How's Henri?" That should have been my first question, but there are so many things I want to know.

"Henri is alive," Mam says, sitting on a sofa with Pap. "He is in the hospital. He is expected to recover."

I breathe a sigh of relief. "Thank God."

Georgie and I sit on a sofa across from Mam and Pap. Mam and Pap haven't let go of each other, and neither have Georgie and I. We are all together, and we're taking no chances. We are alone, the security and Ambassador Hart apparently all giving us a chance to reunite in private.

"What happened at the house?" I ask again.

"It was all rather frightening and chaotic," Mam says. "But eventually, once nearly the town's entire police force showed up, the men gave themselves up and an ambulance crew got in to take care of Henri."

"I'm so sorry you had to go through that," Pap says. "I thought getting you out of the country would keep you safe. I didn't realize they would track you down."

I hang my head. They tracked us down because of my videos. It's all my fault.

"I'm sorry," I say. "I wanted my videos to help save the kingdom. I didn't know they would help them find us."

"But ultimately," Mam says, "those videos saved the day. That's how we found you. The geo-tag on your last video led us to you."

"Really? That's how you found me, Pap? You watched my videos?"

"No, I'm afraid not," Pap says. "The only videos I saw were the ones Felix had his conspirators show me."

Slowly the story unfolds, of how Pap, in hiding in Colsteinburg and unsure who to trust, was presented with the videos that Felix made. With no choice but to try to save my life, Pap flew to Boston, where he was met by Felix, who took him to that office building but didn't tell him I was there. Once Pap had gone off with Felix, Ivan found Mam and Georgie. They spent a sleepless night working with the police and state department trying to locate me. They had the information from my cell phone call to 911, and the police report Bethany and Kim had made, but everything had been a dead end until the video I uploaded. With that final piece of the puzzle, they were able to find me and put the rescue team in place.

A warm feeling of satisfaction goes through me. My videos saved our lives. I did something to save Pap and the country. It's a good thing I never turned off the geo-tagging.

If I still had my phone with me, I'd make a new video, one to let everyone know that I am with Pap and things are finally going in our favor. I wish Felix hadn't smashed my phone, but I suppose if it saved our lives, it was worth the sacrifice.

"Speaking of videos," Georgie says. "Did you see this one?"

She takes out her phone and shows me a video tagged #FeistyFritzi, but it isn't one I made. Instead it's from Bethany, of all people.

"I'm Bethany," she says, "and I thought that princesses were spoiled and just looked out for themselves. I was wrong. To be a princess means to worry about others above yourself. Thank you, Princess Fritzi, for saving my life. Now we must save Fritzi!"

"How did you save her life?" Pap asks, looking at me with a mixture of interest and concern.

"Well, you see, when Felix took me, I escaped. I jumped out of the car and got away."

Georgie squeezes my hand. Pap's eyes fill with pride, Mam's with worry.

"And then I saw Bethany, and when I was talking to her, Felix caught up with me. I ran, but he grabbed Bethany and threatened her. I couldn't let her be hurt because of me, so I went with him. I didn't want to because I knew he wanted to use me to trap Pap, which he did, but I didn't know what else to do."

The next moment, both Mam and Pap are in front of me, holding me.

"You are a brave girl," Mam says, her voice full of love.

"You did the right thing, Fritzi." Pap says, "That girl is right. You know what it means to be a princess. I'm so proud of you."

"Even if it means the end of the kingdom?"

Pap holds my hands in his. "The end of the kingdom is not your fault. If it's anyone's, it's mine. I was not a strong king."

"You talk as if it's over!" I say. "You didn't sign the abdication papers. We can still win."

"This is something I need to discuss with my advisers, and I will. But first, as a family, let's talk about it."

I don't like the sound of that. It sounds like he's willing to give up.

"We can fight for the country, and if I find that there is enough popular support, I will," Pap says. "I will not abandon Colsteinburg because a few people are dissatisfied. By the same token, I will not continue to rule if the majority of people do not want me. I am not, nor do I wish to be, a tyrant."

"But what will we do if you aren't ruling?" I ask. "Where would we live if not in the palace?"

"I'm not sure we'd stay in Colsteinburg if we weren't ruling," Pap answers.

Georgie nods, as if understanding this incredible statement. "It might be awkward," she explains to me. "It would be easier if we weren't there."

I do not agree with that at all, but this probably isn't the time to argue the point.

"But if the people want you to stay king, then you will, right?"

"I will try my best to," Pap answers.

Then I can't stop making the videos. Not yet.

Georgie's phone is in her lap.

"Can I use that to make a video?" I ask. "Felix smashed mine."

"Sure," Georgie says.

"We'll get you a new phone as soon as it is practical," Pap says.

I wonder what it would take for it to be practical. Can we just go shopping today? Are we hiding? What is really going on? Do I even want to worry about that yet?

I turn on the phone's video.

"*Hallo,* Prinzessin Fredericka here."

"And Georgiana," Georgie adds.

I point the camera toward my parents. They grin and join in. "And King Frederick," Pap says.

"Queen Cassandra," Mam adds.

"We are safe now, and all together, and we will come back to Colsteinburg if you want us to. Are you with us? *Prost!*"

Ambassador Hart walks in while I'm uploading the video to my accounts.

"Have you made a lot of these videos?" Pap asks.

"She's been single-handedly convincing the people of Colsteinburg to back the monarchy," Mr. Hart says. "Since she's started posting those videos, there's been a significant turnaround in public opinion. When Orcutt started, he was able to tap into a vein of dissatisfaction, but Fritzi has reminded people about good things. She's given you a fighting chance."

"I did?" I say.

"That's my Fritzi," Pap says, and I feel very proud.

He insists we show them all the videos. I see tears pool in Mam's eyes during some of them. In the end, Pap puts his arm around me.

"I'm very proud of you," he says.

"She's really growing up," Mam says, and she sounds almost sad about it. "I guess I can't think of you as my little girl any longer."

"You can always think of me as your little girl," I promise. I'm not ready to be grown up quite yet.

Out intimate family moment is broken up as more people come into the room. They introduce themselves, and Pap and Mam join them at a conference table. If he's going to stay king, he's got work to do.

"Girls, you may sit with us if you like. This is your future we're discussing," Pap says.

Georgie takes my hand, and together we head to the future, whatever it may bring.

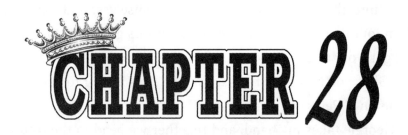

CHAPTER 28

We are going home. That's the one thing I'm able to take away from the meeting at the conference table. It's the only thing that really matters.

Mam and Georgie packed our backpacks before leaving the townhouse, so there is no reason to even go back. The security team escorts us from the building and into a minivan. The van weaves in and out of the city streets and then gets on the highway. I remember the ride from the airport when we first got here and know it shouldn't take long to get there, but instead we seem to be leaving the city behind.

"Where are we going?" I ask, hoping someone in the van can answer and trying to beat down that little bit of fear that tells me these people can't be trusted. What if they are not taking us home, but somewhere else?

"It's fine, Fritzi," Pap says, laying a reassuring hand on my knee. "We're going to the airport I flew into this morning. It's not far."

I relax a bit. I can trust Pap, and he is here with us again, so everything is going to be fine. I don't have to worry anymore.

After about half an hour, we get off the highway and approach a low, modern-looking airport terminal. It is not as big or busy as the airport we flew into, but there are cars picking up and dropping off passengers, and from behind the building, a plane takes off, roaring over our heads.

"Do we have to sit in those tiny little seats again?" I ask.

"Not this time," Pap says, and we are driven straight onto the tarmac, where I see the jet with the red dragon. Our own plane. A burst of happiness surges through me. Things are finally getting back to normal. We board the plane, and I lovingly touch the red leather seats with the royal crest on the headrest. It's almost as good as being home.

"What's our plane doing here?" I ask Pap.

"I needed some way to get to you when they were threatening to kill you. Ivan and I snuck it past the opposition." He takes my backpack from me and stores it in the overhead compartment.

I grin and settle into my seat. Only Pap would think to smuggle out a whole plane!

"Everything's going to be all right now, right?" I ask.

Pap smiles at me, but the smile is sad, and there are lines of stress around his eyes.

"We're all together again, and that is what matters," he answers.

And we are going home. That can't be discounted. We're going home, and the videos I have made will make a difference in convincing everyone that the coup was simply misguided, and then we can all go along as we always have. That's how things have to happen. I'm not ready to imagine any other possibility.

The accumulated stress of the last few days catches up with me, and I fall asleep almost as soon as the plane is in the air. I wake when Georgie nudges me and tells me we are almost home. Out the window, a familiar landscape comes into view: mountains and rivers and valleys. I can't wait to be on the ground and home once more.

The plane lands, and we disembark. There is no welcoming committee, but that is okay. Often we are not met at the airport but take a helicopter to the palace and are greeted there. But there is no helicopter either. Instead, we are met by Marco, the head of security, who hurries us to a nondescript SUV waiting on the tarmac.

Marco drives, and we head toward the city and the palace. An uneasiness begins to creep back in. There is no long motorcade, no official greeting. Things are not as they should be. But then again, we are all disheveled from the past few days. Perhaps it would be better if we didn't make any official appearances until we've had a chance to shower and change.

The ride from the airport is long and uneventful. I lean my

head against the window and relax, drinking in the familiar scenery that I was afraid I would never see again.

The car slows as we get off the highway and enter the city.

I watch the familiar landmarks of Colsteinburg go past. There's the cathedral where I was baptized and where we still go to church. There's the cafe that makes special princess cookies for me and Georgie, and if we go there, they let us give them to any children who come into the store. There's the museum that houses so much of our family history. Just last year, our family portrait was hung there with much fanfare.

There's a difference, though. Instead of the familiar white flag with its red dragon, the green and white flags with the four-sided star are everywhere. It gives me a funny feeling in my stomach, like we're not really home. Or rather, like this isn't home anymore.

As we get closer to the palace, the crowds grow and seem to press in on the car. And despite the windows being tinted, they must be able to see inside, because suddenly crowds surround the car, and we slow to a crawl, nudging past protesters.

Fists pound on the window, and faces loom close, leering at us.

I burrow into Mam's side in an attempt to get as far from the window as I can.

Marco leans on the horn, but he doesn't want to plow the protesters down. Where are the police who should be holding these people back? Is no one on our side anymore?

Outside, the shouts of the protesters are making themselves clearer. Some people are shouting against the monarchy, but I hear other shouts too. Things like "*Vive* King Frederick." So maybe it's not over. Maybe there is hope.

We inch forward, and I'm afraid we'll never make it home, but finally the palace comes into view. My heart lightens when I see the balconies and narrow windows and towers of home. There are crowds here, too, screaming and singing and holding signs, some green and white, others with the familiar red dragon.

This isn't the homecoming I envisioned.

Marco drives into a protected courtyard, and we are able to get out of the car without anyone getting near us, though that doesn't mean we can't see them and hear them holler and shout. Mr. Frank rushes us into the palace, and finally, when the giant door is closed behind us, I can breathe easy again.

We are home. And together. And nothing else matters.

"Can I go up to my room?" I ask as soon as we are inside.

"Of course," Pap says.

I rush up the stairs to my sanctuary and stop dead in the doorway. It's been violated. Trashed. Someone has been in my room. My snow globes are all smashed. The picture of Prince Harry is torn in two.

"Pap!" I scream and run back down the stairs. "Someone was here. They ruined my stuff!"

He catches me in his strong arms and smoothes my hair with his hand. "It's okay. There is no one here now."

"Are you sure?" I ask.

"I'm sure."

I unbury my head from his shirt and look around the main parlor. It has been trashed too, pictures ripped from walls, windows smashed. Furniture overturned and broken. It does not feel like home anymore. It doesn't feel safe.

"What happened?" I ask and see that Pap is looking expectantly at Marco. Apparently, this is a question he already asked before I came downstairs.

"The days were chaotic," Marco explains with a small shrug. "When Orcutt's thugs broke their way in, I did not have enough loyal staff still around to hold them off, and I decided that since the royal family was safe, I would not sacrifice my remaining men to safeguard the building. We let them rampage, and then they left, satisfied with the damage they had done."

"Do we have any staff?" Mam asks, her face looking tight and pinched.

"No one on the premises. There are a few loyal people I can call back now that you are here."

"How safe is it to stay?" Pap asks.

"Orcutt has agreed to a truce while things are sorted out," Marco says. "It should be safe enough, and my staff will secure the perimeter. We will not let anyone in while you are in residence."

I thought when we got home everything would be back to normal. This is not normal, and I don't like it.

"What happens now?" I ask.

"We clean up," Mam says with determination. That's one thing that is good though—Mam has found herself again. "Anyone know where we keep the brooms?"

While I won't argue that having something to do is better than sitting around wallowing in misery, it's heartbreaking to sweep up broken pieces of our former life. Every broken statue and vase and crystal glass makes me crumble a little inside.

Finally, I sink into the sofa and let the tears flow. Pap comes and sits next to me. "What's the matter, Fritzi?" he asks, one arm wrapped around my shoulders.

"I'm hungry. I want everything to be how it was, and I loved that window." I point at the stained glass window of a red dragon that has a hole in the middle where something has been thrown through it.

Pap squeezes me a little, and Mam comes and sits by me as well.

"I loved that window, too," Pap says. "And we'll see if we can find some food. But I can't necessarily make things be how they were before."

"Things are always changing," Mam points out. "Things will never be exactly as they were. They never are, from day to day."

"I don't like change," I say with a pout.

"No one does," Georgie says, leaning on her broom.

Mam laughs. "Most people feel that way sometimes, but you also wouldn't want nothing to ever change. Would you still want to have to go to bed at seven and wear pinafores over your dress at fancy dinners?"

I smile at that. "No, of course not."

"You didn't mind the change when you went off to Academie Sainte Marie," she reminds me.

"True," I say. "Am I going back there?" It hasn't been mentioned, and I've been a little hesitant to bring it up in the middle of everything else.

"Not yet," Mam says. "We need to assess how things stand."

"You mean if Pap is going to stay king."

"Exactly," Mam answers.

I look at Pap. He looks sad and defeated. "It's too soon to say," he says and then stands. "Let's find some food."

Marco has brought some of the staff back, and no sooner do we go looking for food than it turns out the cook has some ready. I convince myself that I'll feel better after I eat.

I don't.

By the evening, Mam's lady maid, Matilde, is back, but not Mademoiselle Colette.

"You're too old for a nanny, anyway," Mam points out as she helps me straighten the mess that is my room.

"I know," I say. That doesn't make me feel better about it.

Over the next couple of days, it becomes obvious that although my videos may have made people nostalgic for the past, Orcutt has won the hearts and minds of the people. Crowds continue to gather and chant outside the palace gates. Less than half the staff has returned, and if the people who knew us best aren't on our side, how can we expect others to be?

Pap calls us all together one afternoon.

"The time has come," he says.

I want to cry out, "No!" That he can't give up. But I can see in his face that he has already accepted the end. Now I suppose it's just up to me to accept it as well.

"Will you all stand beside me when I speak to the people?" he asks.

"Of course," Mam says, laying a hand on his. "We are always beside you, whatever happens."

It's arranged that Pap will make a speech from the central balcony with the TV stations covering it live. Georgie and I dress nicely, in dresses that are neither frilly nor showy but classic and respectful, and we meet our parents by the balcony. Pap wraps us all in a big hug.

"We'll be together," he says. "That's what's important."

It is true, but the knowledge of what we are losing sits on my heart like a rock.

Pap steps out onto the balcony to silence. There are no cheers, but neither are there jeers. The courtyard is full, and people look up expectantly as we join Pap out there.

"My fellow citizens of Colsteinburg," he begins, his voice, with the help of the sound system, reverberating throughout the square. "Eight hundred years ago, my ancestor founded this kingdom. Through that time, the Mohr family has done its best to safeguard Colsteinburg and the people in it. But times change, and it has become obvious that the people of Colsteinburg no longer need our family to safeguard them, nor do they desire that. We respectfully bow to that desire. As of today, we are no longer the royal family of Colsteinburg; we stand before you as fellow citizens. Godspeed, my friends."

He stands for a moment while his speech is met with silence, and then one person starts to clap, and then another. Soon, the whole square is a thunder of applause.

They love us, conditionally.

Pap pulls us all close, and we stand, one last time, on the balcony overlooking our countrymen.

It's not exactly a happy ending.

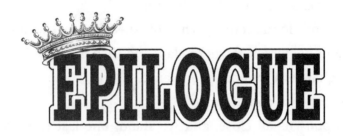

EPILOGUE

Pap rakes leaves in the front yard while I sit on the front step and watch. He looks completely comfortable in jeans and a Harvard sweatshirt, as if he weren't used to wearing a uniform bedecked with medals.

"This is great fun, Fritzi," he says to me. "You should try it. Invigorating. Moves the muscles, and how wonderful to see an accomplishment in a neat pile of leaves."

"I wouldn't want to take the pleasure from you," I say and take a sip from my can of soda. "Besides, we only have one rake."

"An obvious oversight on my part," Pap says. He puts down the rake and comes to sit next to me.

A car pulls up to the curb, and Georgie gets out, waving goodbye to the boy who's dropping her off.

"Who was it this time?" Pap asks.

Georgie grins. "That was Patrick. It's always Patrick these days."

"This week," Pap teases her.

Georgie just tosses her hair and heads inside. She seems to be getting over the loss of Prince Etienne. I wish I could move on quite so easily.

"I miss home," I say.

"I do too," Pap says, putting his hand on my knee. "But I kind of like not having the responsibility for a whole kingdom. It's nice just to have to worry about little things like raking the yard."

I smile. I suppose if Pap can put a positive spin on our new life, I can too.

The house we're renting is on the other side of the school, in a neighborhood of similar houses. It's got a front yard with a white picket fence, something I've been assured is very American. There is a backyard with a flower garden. Inside, we each have our own bedroom again, and although the house isn't large, there is room to spread out.

"It's not so bad," I acknowledge.

"You're making friends," he says, as Jasmine comes into view on her bike.

She stops in front of the house. "Hello, Mr. Moore," she says to Pap. He insists that's what people should call him here, even though it's very strange to my ears. "Want to ride bikes?" she asks me.

"Sure," I say and head to the garage for the bike that Pap bought me last week.

"Don't forget your helmet," Pap calls after me.

I roll my eyes in Jasmine's direction so she will know I think he's terribly overprotective, but I put the helmet on anyway and ride off down the street with her.

This house will never be our palace. America will never be Colsteinburg. But what is it they say, home is where the heart is? I'd say, home is where the family is. My family is here, and that makes it home.

And in my heart, I'll always be a princess.

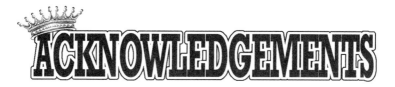

ACKNOWLEDGEMENTS

Writing can be a solitary endeavor, but yet there are so many people who contribute to a finished book.

I'd like to thank my critique partner Tricia Hoover who keeps me on track even from halfway across the country. And also a special thanks to all of my beta readers, especially Jessica Lee Anderson, Kim Baccellia, and Cara Frazier. Thanks also to Rona Gofstein who is always quick with encouragement and advice. A special thanks to Katie Marciniak, daughter extraordinaire, who helps me work through the tough plot points and reminds me to put in question marks where needed. Also a special shout out to my son, Stephen, who happily provides ideas for plot twists, even if most of them don't fit with the vision I have of the story. One day, one of them will, I'm sure.